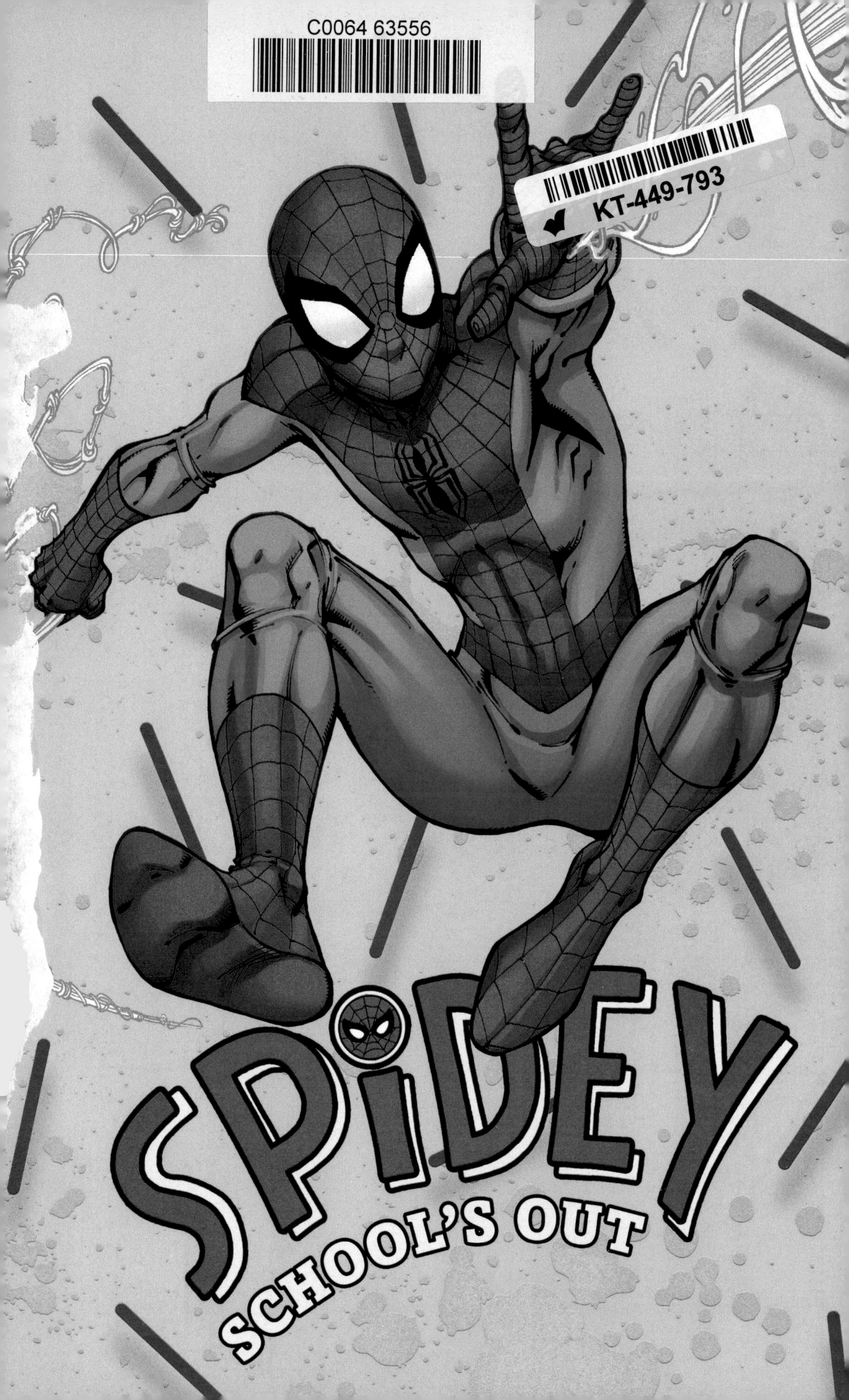
SPIDEY
SCHOOL'S OUT

COLLECTION EDITOR **MARK D. BEAZLEY** · ASSISTANT EDITOR **CAITLIN O'CONNELL**
ASSOCIATE MANAGING EDITOR **KATERI WOODY** · SENIOR EDITOR, SPECIAL PROJECTS **JENNIFER GRÜNWALD**
VP PRODUCTION & SPECIAL PROJECTS **JEFF YOUNGQUIST** · SVP PRINT, SALES & MARKETING **DAVID GABRIEL**
BOOK DESIGNER **JAY BOWEN**

EDITOR IN CHIEF **C.B. CEBULSKI** · CHIEF CREATIVE OFFICER **JOE QUESADA**
PRESIDENT **DAN BUCKLEY** · EXECUTIVE PRODUCER **ALAN FINE**

WHEN HIGH SCHOOL STUDENT PETER PARKER WAS BITTEN BY A RADIOACTIVE SPIDER, HE GAINED THE PROPORTIONAL SPEED, STRENGTH AND AGILITY OF A SPIDER; ADHESIVE FINGERTIPS AND TOES; AND THE UNIQUE PRECOGNITIVE AWARENESS OF DANGER CALLED "SPIDER-SENSE"! AFTER LEARNING THAT WITH GREAT POWER THERE MUST ALSO COME GREAT RESPONSIBILITY, HE BECAME THE CRIMEFIGHTING SUPER HERO CALLED SPIDER-MAN! BUT HE'S NOT A STUDENT OR A SUPER HERO ALL THE TIME, RIGHT? GET READY FOR...

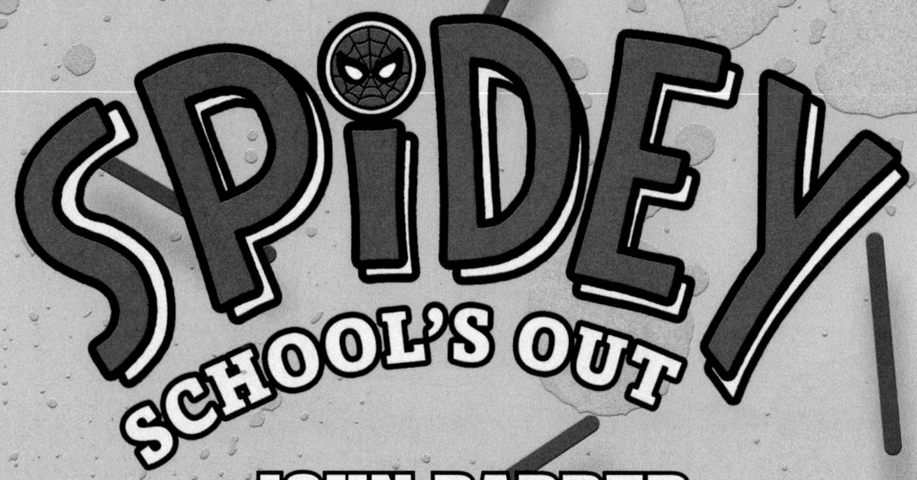

JOHN BARBER
WRITER

TODD NAUCK
ARTIST

RACHELLE ROSENBERG
COLOR ARTIST

COMICRAFT'S JIMMY BETANCOURT
LETTERER

DAVID NAKAYAMA
COVER ART

KATHLEEN WISNESKI
EDITOR

NICK LOWE
SUPERVISING EDITOR

SPIDER-MAN CREATED BY STAN LEE & STEVE DITKO

SPIDEY: SCHOOL'S OUT. First printing 2018. ISBN 978-1-302-91264-2. Published by MARVEL WORLDWIDE, INC., a subsidiary of MARVEL ENTERTAINMENT, LLC. OFFICE OF PUBLICATION: 135 West 50th Street, New York, NY 10020.

Printed in the U.S.A. DAN BUCKLEY, President, Marvel Entertainment; JOHN NEE, Publisher; JOE QUESADA, Chief Creative Officer; TOM BREVOORT, SVP of Publishing; DAVID BOGART, SVP of Business Affairs & Operations, Publishing & Partnership; DAVID GABRIEL, SVP of Sales & Marketing, Publishing; JEFF YOUNGQUIST, VP of Production & Special Projects; DAN CARR, Executive Director of Publishing Technology; ALEX MORALES, Director of Publishing Operations; DAN EDINGTON, Managing Editor; SUSAN CRESPI, Production Manager; STAN LEE, Chairman Emeritus. For information regarding advertising in Marvel Comics or on Marvel.com, please contact Vit DeBellis, Custom Solutions & Integrated Advertising Manager, at vdebellis@marvel.com. For Marvel subscription inquiries, please call 888-511-5480. **Manufactured between 9/28/2018 and 10/30/2018 by QUAD GRAPHICS SARATOGA, SARATOGA SPRINGS, NY, USA.**

10 9 8 7 6 5 4 3 2 1

1
WELCOME TO
STARK
CAMP

I REALLY DON'T HAVE TIME FOR THIS TODAY.
DON'T GET ME WRONG. POWER, RESPONSIBILITY, ALL THAT STUFF--I KNOW.
BUT SOMETIMES BEING A HERO CAN GET IN THE WAY.
OH, HEY--I DIDN'T EVEN INTRODUCE MYSELF. SEE WHAT I MEAN?
I'M YOUR FRIENDLY NEIGHBORHOOD SPIDER-MAN--BUT YOU CAN CALL ME
SPIDEY
AND LIKE I SAID-- DON'T GET ME WRONG.
NO MATTER HOW LATE I'M RUNNING...

...I'LL NEVER LEAVE ANYBODY HANGING.
GOT 'EM!
HERE YOU ARE, MA'AM! ONE SET OF LOST HOUSE KEYS, COURTESY OF YOUR FRIENDLY NE--
HE'S STEALING MY KEYS!
THEY'RE RIGHT ABOUT YOU! YOU'RE A MENACE!
LADY--I'M JUST TRYING TO HELP!
THE WEBBING WILL COME OFF IN A COUPLE HOURS.
A COUPLE HOURS?! I NEED TO GO HOME NOW!
I HAFTA TAKE MY MEDICINE!
I LOVE THIS CITY.
I CAN CALL YOU A LOCK--
OW!
WHAP
--SMITH! I WAS JUST TRYING TO HELP!
THE STORY OF MY LIFE.

I WONDER WHERE SHE GOT THE IDEA I'M A MENACE.
SPIDER-MAN: MENACE
DAILY BUGLE
On sale daily
I NEED TO WORK ON MY IMAGE. PLUS MAYBE MY SUPER HERO SKILLS...
...I MEAN, SOMETIMES I CAN HOLD MY OWN WITH IRON MAN, BLACK PANTHER, CAPTAIN AMERICA--ALL THOSE GUYS...
...BUT OTHER DAYS I FEEL LIKE I'M JUST SPRAYING A BUNCH OF WEBS AT THE PROBLEM.
BUT, HEY. IT GOT ME THIS FAR.
SO, YOU ASK,* WHY AM I IN SUCH A RUSH?
I'LL TELL YOU. THIS IS THE BEST DAY OF THE SCHOOL YEAR...
...BECAUSE IT'S THE LAST DAY OF THE SCHOOL YEAR.
*OR I HOPE YOU DO, ANYWAY.

"BUT, PETER," YOU SAY...

..BECAUSE YOU KNOW I'M REALLY PETER PARKER...

...MILD-MANNERED HIGH SCHOOL STUDENT...

..."I THOUGHT YOU LIKED SCHOOL."

PETER-- RUSHING AROUND WON'T MAKE THE DAY GO FASTER.

YOU KNOW WHAT YOU SIGNED UP FOR WHEN YOU STARTED DATING HIM, GWEN.

I DO LIKE SCHOOL. MOSTLY.

BUT THIS YEAR'S GOT SOMETHING SPECIAL.

ONCE TODAY ENDS...

...SUMMER BEGINS.

I KNOW EVERY YEAR IS LIKE THAT BUT--

GOTTA GO. I'LL EXPLAIN LATER.
RINNG

OKAY, GUYS. IT'S BEEN A HECK OF A YEAR.

PETER, WAIT!

YOU TOLD ME TO WARN YOU WHEN YOU ACT WEIRD, PETE...

JUST HURRY UP, GUYS--

"--I CAN'T BE LATE!"
YOU ARE RIDICULOUS, PETE.
THE ONLY GUY I KNOW WHO CAN'T WAIT TO GET OUT OF SCHOOL...
...JUST SO HE CAN GO TO ANOTHER SCHOOL.
HARRY, IT'S NOT A-- IT'S A STARK TECHNOLOGY CAMP.
WHAT AM I SUPPOSED TO DO NEXT WEEK? JUST HAVE FUN WITHOUT YOU DRAGGING ME DOWN WITH YOUR ENNUI AND NERVOUSNESS?
THANKS, GWEN. THIS IS A BIG HONOR. ONLY, LIKE, TWENTY KIDS GET TO GO.
AND THE COOL PART IS IT'S ALL SCIENCE AND TECHNOLOGY, NOT THE BORING STUFF.
THERE'S MORE TO LIFE THAN BUNSEN BURNERS AND...
...WHATEVER ELSE YOU LIKE.
I'M EXCITED TO MEET A BUNCH OF SMART PEOPLE WHO SHARE MY INTERESTS. YOU KNOW IT'S HARD FOR ME TO MAKE FRIENDS.
I WONDER WHY.
I MEAN BESIDES YOU TWO.
OH, PETER...
HI, AUNT MAY!
...IF YOU WANT TO GET THERE IN TIME FOR TONY STARK'S SPEECH...

"...WE'D BETTER GET A MOVE ON."
AFTER ALL, I COULDN'T LET MY FAVORITE NEPHEW GO TO CAMP ALONE.
I'M YOUR ONLY NEPHEW.
YOU DON'T KNOW WHAT I GET UP TO IN MY SPARE TIME.
I COULD'VE TAKEN THE SUBWAY.
OR WEBLINES.
WHICH IS PROBABLY WHY I EVEN GOT ACCEPTED. SEE, IRON MAN AND ME TEAMED UP LAST YEAR.
TONY STARK MUST HAVE FIGURED OUT WHO I AM AND GOT ME INTO HIS CAMP AS A REWARD.
NOT THAT I'M COMPLAINING.
CALL ME WHEN YOU'RE SETTLED IN, AND I'LL SEE YOU NEXT FRIDAY, PETER.
OKAY, AUNT MAY!
I LOVE YOU, PETER!
YOU TOO, MAY.
I MEAN, COME ON. OPPORTUNITIES LIKE THIS ONLY HAPPEN SO OFTEN...

...YOU GOTTA TAKE ADVANTAGE.
NICE SUITCASE.
THWAP
UH. THANKS?
AFTER ALL...

...THINGS *THIS GOOD* JUST DON'T USUALLY HAPPEN TO ME.
WELCOME TO STARK CAMP
PETER... WE'RE *HOME.*

HI.
...
I'M PETER.
OKAY.

UH. WELL, WHAT'S YOUR NAME?
MY FRIENDS CALL ME GG.
GREAT. SO, GG--
GLORIANA.

RIGHT. OKAY.
ANYWAY, I JUST GOT HERE, AND I'M NOT QUITE SURE WHERE TO GO. SEE, I--
TEK

AHH!
WALL!
UH. WALL?
SO THE RUMORS ARE TRUE--
--THEY DID LOWER ADMISSION STANDARDS THIS YEAR.
TRY THE ELEVATOR, GENIUS. AND CHECK YOUR EMAIL FOR YOUR DORM ASSIGNMENT.
OOOH, THAT'S RIGHT. I HAVE A ROOMMATE. AT LEAST HE'S PROBABLY GOING TO BE MORE FRIENDLY...

...I MEAN...HE HAS TO BE, RIGHT?
HI.
I'M PETE. PETER. PETE. EITHER ONE'S OKAY.
I'M YOUR ROOMMATE.
UH. HI?
GREAT. NOW IT'S THE SILENT TREATMENT.
WHAT'S WITH EVERYBODY HERE?
BEING INTO SCIENCE DOESN'T MEAN YOU HAVE TO BE A--
HEY... WHO'S THERE?

OH WOW! YOU MUST BE MY ROOMMATE! SORRY I DIDN'T HEAR YOU!
I WAS LISTENING TO A BRUCE BANNER PODCAST. YOU KNOW HOW THAT GOES, RIGHT?
I'M GANKE!
OH, AH, I'M PETER.
THAT'S SO COOL!
IT IS?
IS IT NOT?
SORRY ABOUT THE MESS.
YOU'RE NEW HERE, RIGHT? I MEAN, I KNOW YOU'RE NEW. IF YOU'D BEEN HERE, I'D HAVE SEEN YOU. BECAUSE I'VE BEEN HERE.
YOU'RE THE FIRST FRIENDLY FACE I'VE SEEN.
STARK CAMP CAN BE WEIRD AT FIRST. EVERYBODY SPENDS TOO MUCH TIME WITH THEIR DEAL.
THEIR "DEAL"?
THE THING THEY DO. I LIKE COMPUTERS. YOU MEET GG?
SORTA.
SHE LIKES VIDEO GAMES. EVERYBODY WORKS ON A PROJECT BASED ON THEIR--
WAIT A MINUTE! WHAT TIME IS IT?! WE'RE LATE!
I THINK I FOUND A KINDRED SPIRIT AT LAST.
COME ON--

"--YOU DON'T WANNA MISS TONY STARK!"
I CAN SEE YOU'RE A BRIGHT GROUP OF KIDS THIS YEAR.
EVER SINCE I TOLD THE WORLD I'M IRON MAN, APPLICATIONS HAVE GONE THROUGH THE ROOF--AND TRUST ME, I'VE CRASHED THROUGH ENOUGH ROOFS TO KNOW...
...TO KNOW...

...WHO WRITES THIS STUFF?
YOU KNOW WHAT? LET ME LEVEL WITH YOU. IT'S HARD TO GET IN TO STARK CAMP, SO IF YOU'RE HERE, YOU'RE REAL SMART.
I LIKE SMART KIDS. I WANT TO ENCOURAGE SMART KIDS.

I GOT LUCKY--MY FOLKS WERE WELL-OFF.
NOT EVERYBODY HAS THAT, SO I DO WHAT I CAN TO LEVEL THE PLAYING FIELD. BECAUSE YOU--
--ARE GONNA MAKE THE FUTURE.

ME?
HE'S POINTING RIGHT AT ME!
COME ON, TONY. I'M TRYING TO MAKE A GOOD IMPRESSION WITH THESE KIDS.
DO YOU HAVE TO SINGLE ME OUT?

AND IF YOU TRY HARD, DO YOUR BEST, AND MAYBE CATCH SOME GOOD BREAKS--
--WHEN IT COMES TO WHAT YOU CAN DO--

--THE SKY'S THE LIMIT. AND I SHOULD KNOW!
DID I REALLY SAY THAT OUT LOUD? FRIDAY, TAKE A MEMO--FIND NEW WRITERS FOR THESE THINGS.
YES, SIR.

WOW! TONY STARK! IRON MAN! THAT'S SO GREAT!
IT WAS A HOLOGRAM. I THOUGHT HE'D BE HERE.
YEAH-- WHAT'S WITH HIM? HOLOGRAMS ARE MY DEAL.
WELL, I THINK YOUR BRICK WALL IS REALLY COOL, G--GLORIANA.
SERIOUSLY? YOU THINK I'M MAKING BRICK WALLS?
YOU--UH, YOU...AREN'T YOU? I WASN'T TRYING TO--
HEY, PETE!
THESE ARE THE TWINS, NEEL AND RIYA.
HEY.
YO.

YOU'RE EDITING DNA?!
NO, NO--WE'RE TRYING TO TURN OFF GENES THAT TRIGGER CANCER PROLIFERATION.
WE'RE SIMULATING IT, ANYWAY--THIS IS JUST A DIGITAL PROOF OF CONCEPT. WE'RE FIFTEEN. WE DON'T HAVE ACTUAL NANO-MACHINES.
LET ME GUESS. IS IT TO MAKE SUPER-POWERS? GIVE PEOPLE ENHANCED ABILITIES LIKE THE AVENGERS?
UH, LET'S GO OVER HERE-- YOU'LL WANT TO MEET CINDY. SHE'S--
WAIT, WHAT ABOUT THESE GUYS? I RAN INTO ONE OF THEM OUTSIDE.
WHAT'S THEIR DEAL...?

GLAD YOU ASKED. I'M ETHAN AND THAT'S LACHLAN.
WE'RE PRODUCING A MOBILE APP THAT'S GOING TO REALLY PIVOT THE MARKET.
IT'S CALLED KILLBLAST TRIGGER-- IN A POSTAPOCALYPTIC LANDSCAPE, THE ONLY WAY TO STAY ALIVE--
--IS TO CONNECT THREE OR MORE BLAST-BLOCKS. BUT THE BEAUTY IS, IF YOU GET STUCK--
AND YOU WILL-- ROUGHLY EVERY 186 SECONDS OF PLAYTIME.
--SWIPING LEFT WILL TRIGGER A MICROTRANSACTION FROM YOUR KILLBLAST WALLET.
ER... HOW MUCH MONEY...?
THAT DEPENDS ON TRAFFIC--COULD BE A LITTLE AS A FEW CENTS, COULD BE UP TO $12 A SWIPE.
WE ONLY NEED PARENTAL AUTHORIZATION ONCE, AND THE WALLET STAYS OPEN UNTIL SOMEBODY ACTIVELY CLOSES IT.
WAIT-- YOU'RE STEALING FROM KIDS?
THAT'S... HORRIBLE.
OH, YEAH, WELL, LET ME TAKE BUSINESS ADVICE FROM A KID WITH A SECONDHAND SUITCASE THAT LOOKS LIKE IT ALMOST SURVIVED WORLD WAR I.
IT WAS MY UNCLE'S.
I WANT TO LAY INTO THESE GUYS--
--BUT I CATCH SOMETHING OUT OF THE CORNER OF MY EYE.
I KNOW THAT JACKET...
...AND THE GAUNTLET. THAT'S NO SCIENCE PROJECT...

...AND I HAVE A FEELING I'M ABOUT TO BE LATE *AGAIN.*
HEY--*PETE!* DON'T *LISTEN* TO THESE *GUYS!*
COME BACK!
I'VE BEEN DOING THE *SUPER HERO THING* LONG ENOUGH TO KNOW THAT A *TECHNOLOGY CARNIVAL* IS LIKE A...
...*UH*...
...*RED CAPE* WAVING AT THE *BULL* OF *CRIMINALITY*...?
OKAY. MY *ANALOGIES* NEED WORK.
HEY. HAVEN'T WE *MET* SOMEWHERE BEFORE?
WHAT?
SPIDER-MAN!
TZZZATT
WATHOOM
WHAT WAS THAT?
ONE WAY TO FIND OUT.

I'M HAPPY YOU REMEMBER ME--BUT I GOTTA ADMIT, I'M HAVING TROUBLE WITH YOU...
...I KNOW YOU'RE NOT ELECTRO, EVEN IF YOU HAVE HIS ELECTRICAL BLAST THING GOING ON.
I THINK YOUR NAME'S SOMETHING WITH ELECTRICITY, THOUGH...
ELEKTRA?
CABLE?
THWIP
SPLATT
SHOCK--URF!
SHOCKURF. THAT'S IT! NOW I REMEMBER.
OKAY, POSSIBLY BLINDING THE GUY BLASTING ZILLIONS* OF VOLTS WHILE I'M BELITTLING HIM IS POTENTIALLY NOT A GREAT IDEA.
*A NUMBER REACHED BY CAREFUL SCIENTIFIC CALCULATION.

BUT, HEY, AT LEAST NOBODY'S AROUND.
WE GOTTA SEE THIS!
CAREFUL, YOU GUYS. MY MOM WOULD KILL ME IF I DIED ON THE FIRST DAY OF CAMP.
HEY, SHOCKER!*
HOW'S YOUR RADAR SENSE? THAT'S YOU, RIGHT?
*YEAH, YEAH, I REMEMBER HIS NAME IRL.
THIS WASN'T SUPPOSED TO BE A FIGHT, SPIDER-MAN!
THEN DO I HAVE GOOD NEWS FOR YOU!
WHEN I GET MY HANDS ON YOU, IT WON'T BE A FIGHT.
BRAVE TALK, BUT PRIORITY NUMBER ONE IS PROTECTING MY CLASSMATES.
I DON'T INTEND TO GET TO THE HEAD OF THE CLASS BY LETTING THE COMPETITION GET FRIED.

I MADE SURE NOBODY'S INSIDE.
HONEST.
WANTON DESTRUCTION OF PUBLIC PROPERTY LIKE THIS IS WHY PEOPLE HATE ME, ISN'T IT?
STILL, HE'S SHOOTING BLIND. THE WEBS SHOULD KEEP HIM THAT WAY FOR A COUPLE HOURS--
--UNLESS HE RUNS A CURRENT OF ABOUT 100VDC, WHICH I SUPPOSE MAYBE COULD MAKE THE WEBLINE LOSE ADHESION...
YOU LEARN SOMETHING NEW EVERY DAY AT SCIENCE CAMP.
YOU THINK YOU CAN STOP ME, SPIDER-MAN?! WELL, NOTHING STOPS THE SHOCK--
--ER.
WHERE DID THIS COME FROM?!
GIVE UP, SHOCKER! WE HAVE YOU SURROUNDED!
DON'T SAY "WITH BRICKS." THAT'S NOT A JOKE. IT DOESN'T MAKE SENSE. DON'T SAY--
WITH BRICKS!
UGH. SOMETIMES MY MOUTH HAS A MIND OF ITS OWN.

I DON'T HEAR HIM.
IT'S NOT GOING TO TAKE LONG UNTIL HE FIGURES OUT THAT WALL'S NOT REAL.
I GOT HIM-- YOU CAN TURN OFF THE BRICK PROJECTOR.
IT'S NOT A BRICK PROJECTOR! THERE'S A LOT MORE TO IT THAN THAT!

AW.

HEY, SPIDER-MAN. YOU GONNA FOLLOW HIM OR WHAT?
ONE--IT SMELLS TERRIBLE DOWN THERE.
TWO-- THERE'S NO WAY TO KNOW WHERE HE WENT.

THAT'S COOL, SPIDER-MAN! YOU STILL SAVED THE DAY.
I HAD HELP.
LEMME GET A PICTURE!

NO, HANG ON-- THAT USUALLY TURNS OUT BAD.
CLICK
ARE YOU KIDDING? THIS'LL LOOK GREAT ON OUR APP STOREFRONT!
SHEESH. I'VE HAD IT WITH TODAY.
STAY SAFE, KIDS. AND HAVE FUN IN CAMP.
OR WHATEVER YOU'RE DOING. I DON'T KNOW WHAT YOU'RE DOING, I JUST GUESSED CAMP.
THAT IS AMAZING! SPIDER-MAN! THAT'S ALMOST AS GOOD AS SEEING A HOLOGRAM OF AN AVENGER, RIGHT, PETE?
UH... PETE?
WHERE ARE YOU, BUDDY?
OH NO. I CAN'T GO HOME...I'M STAYING HERE.
WITH GANKE, WHO'S ALREADY LOOKING FOR ME AFTER I RAN OUTSIDE LITERALLY SECONDS BEFORE SPIDER-MAN SHOWED UP.
OFF TO A GOOD START, PETER...

...NOWHERE TO GO BUT UP.
WHAT KIND OF A MANIAC PUTS A SECRET HEADQUARTERS IN A SEWER?
BEGGARS CAN'T BE CHOOSERS, SHOCKER...
...AND NEITHER CAN VULTURES.
I HOPE YOU GOT THE PICTURES OF THE STARK CENTER.
OUR CLIENTS WANT NEW WEAPONS FOR A NEW SEASON... SO I'D LIKE TO GET OUR CATALOG UP AND RUNNING.
AFTER ALL-- WE HAVE TO KNOW WHAT WE NEED TO STEAL.

2

I KNOW WHAT YOU'RE THINKING.
"WHAT A HERO--SELFLESSLY PATROLLING THE STREETS OF NEW YORK, ON THE LOOKOUT FOR CRIMINAL ACTIVITY.
"WE COULD ALL LEARN A LITTLE SOMETHING FROM--
AW, WHO AM I KIDDING?
YOU PROBABLY THINK I JUST KIDNAPPED YOUR CAT OR SOMETHING, BECAUSE EVERYBODY ALWAYS THINKS THE WORST OF ME.
SPIDER-MAN WAS TRYIN' TO STEAL STUFF, FOR SURE...
SEE?
...LIKE, YOU THINK HE JUST HAPPENED TO BE HANGIN' 'ROUND WHEN SHOCKER SHOWED UP?
YOU THINK THEY WERE IN CAHOOTS.
Y'TOOK THE WORDS RIGHT OUTTA MY MOUTH--
--SPIDER-MAN AIN'T A HERO LIKE IRON MAN, THAT'S FOR SURE.
THE GUARD'S ACTUALLY GOT A POINT.

IRON MAN NEVER HAD TO HIDE OUT UNTIL NIGHTFALL TO SNEAK BACK INTO HIS DORM ROOM--
--BECAUSE HE'S SUDDENLY FOUND HIMSELF IN A SUMMER CAMP--
--TRYING TO KEEP HIS IDENTITY SECRET FROM HIS NEW ROOMMATE.
OR, IF IRON MAN EVER DID DO THAT, WE HAVE AN AMAZING COINCIDENCE ON OUR HANDS.
GANKE CAN QUESTION ME ALL HE WANTS IN THE MORNING, JUST AS LONG AS I CAN EXPERIENCE A FEW HOURS OF THE BLISSFUL OBLIVION OF SLEE--
WHAT DO YOU THINK YOU'RE DOING?!
SNEAKING INTO OUR ROOM IN THE MIDDLE OF THE NIGHT AFTER A SUPER VILLAIN ATTACK?
YOU TRYING TO HIDE FROM ME?

UH. GANKE.
HEKNOWSI'M SPIDEYHE KNOWSI'M
I JUST DIDN'T WANT TO WAKE YOU UP AND--

I WAS SO WORRIED ABOUT YOU.
UH. THANKS?
YOU SHOULDN'T BE EMBARRASSED ABOUT RUNNING HOME JUST BECAUSE SPIDER-MAN AND ELECTRO STARTED THROWING STUFF AROUND.
I THINK THAT WAS THE SHOCKER, NOT THAT I'M AN EXPERT OR ANYTHING. ALSO--
--WHAT?!
I'M GLAD YOU'RE BACK. IT'S BEEN CHAOS!
THE ADULTS THINK SPIDER-MAN WAS BEHIND EVERYTHING.
SO I HEARD... WAIT...
...YOU DON'T?
ARE YOU KIDDING? EVERYBODY IN CAMP KNOWS SPIDEY STOPPED THE BAD GUY.
SO YOU-- THEY--YOU ALL THINK SPIDER-MAN IS A HERO?
TYPICAL...
...I STOP ELECTRIC MAN, BUT MR. TIGHTS GETS ALL THE CREDIT.
GLORIANA!
IS EVERYBODY STILL UP?

WHO COULD SLEEP AFTER A DAY LIKE THAT?!
AND EVEN IF SPIDER-MAN GETS THE ACHIEVEMENT TROPHIES, MRS. LIU HAS TO KNOW MY INVENTION DROVE THE BAD PERSON AWAY.
WHICH PUTS ME IN FIRST PLACE HEADING INTO THE WEEKEND.
WAIT, WAIT-- SPIDER-MAN DIDN'T--
--FIRST PLACE IN WHAT?
WHO'S MRS. LIU?
DAY AFTER TOMORROW'S WHEN WE PRESENT OUR PROJECT STATUS REPORTS TO THE GROUP.
GG'S BEEN WORKING ON HERS SINCE MIDDLE SCHOOL, BUT EVERY YEAR MRS. LIU PICKS SOMEBODY ELSE TO GET THE STARK CUP.
EVERYBODY NOT ONLY KNOWS THEIR PROJECTS BUT THEY'VE BEEN WORKING ON THEM FOR YEARS?!
WELL, YOU GOT ACCEPTED, WHAT, SIX MONTHS AGO? I BET YOU CAME UP WITH A GREAT PLAN.
GET SOME SLEEP, PETE. CAN'T WAIT TO SEE WHAT YOUR DEAL IS.
THAT MAKES TWO OF US.
I GUESS I SHOULD HAVE READ MY ACCEPTANCE LETTER A LITTLE CLOSER.
SO I HAVE TWO DAYS TO FIGURE OUT MY DEAL AND COME UP WITH A PROJECT...
...PLUS THE SHOCKER IS STILL OUT THERE SOMEWHERE.
REMEMBER THE OLD DAYS, WHEN I BELIEVED IN THE BLISSFUL OBLIVION OF SLEEP?

BLAST IT!
SMASH IT!
WRECK IT!
BLOW AWAY THE COMPETITION LIKE A SUPER HERO--

KILLBLAST TRIGGER
--KILLBLAST TRIGGER MAKES YOU THE BLAST MASTER!
WHAT IS THAT SUPPOSED TO BE?

STREET CRED.
OKAY, I GET PEOPLE HERE LIKE HIM, BUT EVERYBODY ELSE HATES SPIDER-MAN.
PARENTS HATE HIM. THAT MAKES HIM COOL, PETE. DID YOU JUST LAND ON PLANET EARTH?
WOW...IF THIS IS WHAT EARTH LOOKS LIKE--THEN YEAH, I'VE NEVER BEEN HERE BEFORE.
IS...IS THAT AN ARC REACTOR?
STARK ALWAYS HAS THE BEST STUFF. I KNOW BECAUSE I ALWAYS GET THE BEST STUFF AND THIS STUFF IS BETTER.
MY WHOLE LIFE, I'VE BEEN SCROUNGING FOR EVERYTHING...
PETER PARKER, DUMPSTER DIVER--

--I HAD YOU PEGGED THE SECOND I SAW YOU WITH YOUR GRANDPA'S SUITCASE.
WAP
IT WAS MY UNCLE'S--
DID YOU RUN TO YOUR UNCLE'S HOUSE WHILE WE WERE HANGING WITH SPIDER-MAN?
YOU WEREN'T--
--I MEAN, YEAH, I JUST BET SPIDER-MAN LIKES YOUR STUPID CELL PHONE GAME.
KILLBLAST TRIGGER'S NOT JUST A GAME, IT'S A LIFESTYLE. AND SPIDEY KNOWS A GOOD THING--WE GOT HIS PIC ALL OVER BRAAP AND FRINGO.
WHO?
SOCIAL MEDIA. LOOK INTO IT--MAYBE SOMEBODY WILL ACCIDENTALLY LIKE YOU.
ARE THOSE REAL THINGS, GANKE? HAVE YOU--
ARRRRGHH!
NONE OF THIS IS COMPILING RIGHT!
THE PROCESSOR SHOULDN'T BE USING THAT MUCH POWER!
I SPENT EVERY STUPID WEEKEND THIS STUPID YEAR WRITING STUPID CODE...

HI. UH, PETER. I MEAN, I'M PETER. FROM LAST NIGHT? IN CASE YOU DIDN'T REMEMBER ME.
ANYTHING I CAN DO TO HELP?
NOT UNLESS YOU HAVE A SPARE DXS-6502 WITH A PARALLEL L TERMINAL.
I DO NOT HAVE ONE.
NOT A SPARE ONE, ANYWAY.
LOOK, I'M SURE YOU'LL FIGURE OUT YOUR BRICK WALL THING.
I DON'T KNOW HOW MR. STARK LET YOU IN HERE.
THIS IS AN IMMERSIVE GAMING EXPERIENCE IN REALSPACE. 3D VR WITH NO HEADSET.
SO YOU'RE SAYING IT'S...NOT A BRICK WALL PROJECTOR...?
WORLDCRAFTING IS A LOT MORE THAN WALLS.
YOU CAN BUILD ANY STRUCTURE YOU CAN IMAGINE, ALL OUT OF INTERCHANGEABLE HOLOGRAPHIC VOXELS.
YOU CAN SAVE AND TRADE YOUR CREATIONS ONLINE.
THAT'S... PRETTY NEAT, ACTUALLY.
WAIT'LL YOU SEE THIS...

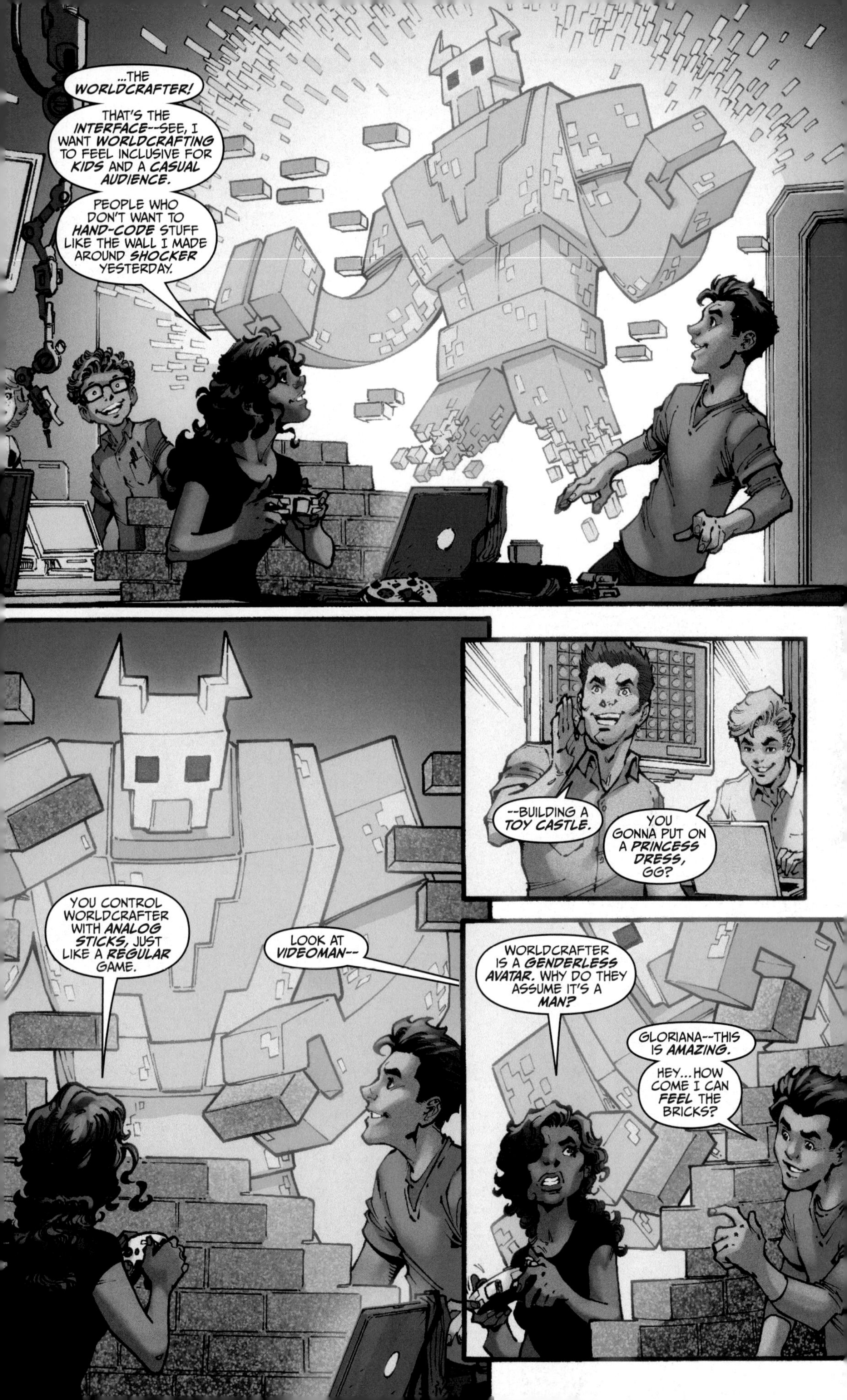
...THE WORLDCRAFTER!
THAT'S THE INTERFACE--SEE, I WANT WORLDCRAFTING TO FEEL INCLUSIVE FOR KIDS AND A CASUAL AUDIENCE.
PEOPLE WHO DON'T WANT TO HAND-CODE STUFF LIKE THE WALL I MADE AROUND SHOCKER YESTERDAY.
YOU CONTROL WORLDCRAFTER WITH ANALOG STICKS, JUST LIKE A REGULAR GAME.
LOOK AT VIDEOMAN--
--BUILDING A TOY CASTLE.
YOU GONNA PUT ON A PRINCESS DRESS, GG?
WORLDCRAFTER IS A GENDERLESS AVATAR. WHY DO THEY ASSUME IT'S A MAN?
GLORIANA--THIS IS AMAZING.
HEY...HOW COME I CAN FEEL THE BRICKS?

THE PROJECTOR EMITS A LOW-LEVEL ELECTROMAGNETIC FIELD TO REPEL OBJECTS--AND PEOPLE.
THE TACTILE FEEDBACK RIFFS ON OLD REPULSOR TECHNOLOGY--
--NO ARC REACTOR OR ANYTHING, JUST KINDA THE SAME IDEA.
I'VE--UH-- SEEN IRON MAN USE REPULSORS. AREN'T THEY DANGEROUS?
PEOPLE KEEP SAYING THAT, BUT THE SYSTEM CAN'T PRODUCE ENOUGH FORCE TO DO MORE THAN TINGLE.
I DON'T KNOW...
THERE'S NO DIAL ON THE BACK THAT GOES BETWEEN GOOD AND EVIL. I'M VERY THOROUGH.
VIDEOMAN-- UGH, I MEAN WORLDCRAFTER-- IS COMPLETELY IN MY...
...UH...
THAT'S WEIRD.

SCRASH
AHH!
LOOK OUT!
I DIDN'T MAKE IT DO THAT! THAT WASN'T ME!
NEEL, RIYA--ARE YOU OKAY?
TURN IT OFF!
WHAT DO YOU THINK I'M TRYING TO DO?! THERE'S NO WAY THIS CAN BE HAPPENING!
I HATE TO BREAK IT TO YOU, BUT--
I MEAN, WORLDCRAFTER SHOULD JUST VANISH IF THE CONTROLLER STOPS WORKING!
WELL, THERE'S ONE WAY TO MAKE ANY VIDEO GAME CHARACTER VANISH--

--I DO BELIEVE THEY ALL NEED A LITTLE THING CALLED...
POINK
...ELECTRICITY!
ROOO111RRR!
SCRACCH
WHY DIDN'T THAT WORK?
WHAT PART OF DXS-6502 WITH A PARALLEL L TERMINAL DID YOU NOT UNDERSTAND?
LIKE 90 PERCENT OF IT?
IT'S A BATTERY!
THE SYSTEM HAS A BATTERY BACKUP!
YOU ARE THOROUGH. HOW LONG WILL IT LAST?
NORMALLY EIGHT HOURS--BUT WITH THE POWER SURGING, I'D SAY IT'S CUT DOWN TO MAYBE...THREE AND A HALF?
WELL, THAT'S GOOD NEWS. EIGHT HOURS OF THIS WOULD BE DIFFICULT.

TIME FOR PETER PARKER TO MAKE A GRACEFUL--
YAAAAAHHH!
--EXIT.
WELL, ANY EXIT YOU CAN WALK AWAY FROM...
THAT THING KILLED PETE!
OR MY EXIT CREATES A WHOLE NEW SET OF PROBLEMS.
ROOO10O111GH!
PETER-- DON'T BE DEAD!
I KNOW WE JUST MET BUT YOU SEEMED COOL AND I KNOW YOU'RE NOT GOING TO BELIEVE THIS BUT BACK HOME I DON'T ACTUALLY HAVE A LOT OF IRL FRIENDS AND...
...AND...
...PETE!
YOU'RE OKAY!

THE KID'S FINE. NOW, THIS COMPUTER THING, ON THE OTHER HAND...
...IT'S IN FOR A WORLD OF TROUBLE.
SO HERE'S MY THINKING.
THERE WAS JUST A BREAK-IN, SO IT MAKES SENSE FOR SPIDER-MAN TO BE NEARBY. THE PROBLEM IS--WHERE DOES PETER PARKER GO?
SO I CAME UP WITH A QUICK AND DIRTY SOLUTION.
HE WON'T STAND UP TO SCRUTINY--BUT AS LONG AS I KEEP MOVING, WEBBY SHOULD WORK JUST FINE.
I JUST HOPE THE WEBS COME OUT SO AUNT MAY DOESN'T KILL ME.
NOW TO SWOOP IN AND SAVE THE DAY AGAIN. THESE KIDS ALREADY THINK--
--I MEAN, THEY KNOW--
--SPIDER-MAN IS A HERO...
THWIP
...BUT HERE'S A PRETTY GREAT CHANCE TO PROVE IT TO THE--
WUNK
OOPS.
PETE! YOU'RE DEAD AGAIN!
SPIDER-MAN JUST KILLED PETER PARKER!

NO! HE'S-- I MEAN, YOU'RE TALKING ABOUT THAT KID I JUST SAVED?
I DIDN'T KNOW HIS NAME UNTIL RIGHT THIS MOMENT.
IT WAS PETE UNTIL YOU MURDERED HIM!
HE'S FINE! MY SPIDEY-SENSE SAYS HE'S FINE.
LUCKY FOR ME, GANKE DOESN'T KNOW THAT'S NOT HOW SPIDER-SENSE WORKS.
IT ACTUALLY JUST TELLS ME WHEN I'M IN IMMINENT DANGER, LIKE...
...LIKE WHEN SPIDEY'S SUDDEN APPEARANCE MAKES THE BAD GUY TOTALLY LOSE IT.
UFFF.
SPIDEY! CAN WE GET ANOTHER PIC? THE LAST ONE GOT 4,000 GRABS ON GRABBIT!
I COMPLETELY KNOW WHAT THAT IS, BECAUSE I'M SO EXTRA WHEN IT COMES TO CURRENT STUFF.
THWIP

ROO101RR!
VWIPP
HEY! NO FAIR! YOU CAN'T--
OKAY, OKAY, MAYBE YOU CAN-- BUT LET'S SEE YOU TRY THAT TWICE!

IT'S HIM, MRS. LIU--THE GUY IN THE BLUE-AND-RED TIGHTS.
I KNOW WHO SPIDER-MAN IS! WHAT'S GOING ON?!
HE KILLED PETER PARKER.
JUST LAST NIGHT GANKE WAS ON MY SIDE.
I'M STARTING TO THINK I HAVE AN IMAGE PROBLEM.
BUT IMMEDIATE PROBLEMS FIRST.
LOOKS LIKE VIDEOMAN CAN PULL OFF THAT BODY-SPLITTING TRICK MORE THAN ONCE... BUT MAYBE I'M GOING ABOUT THIS THE WRONG WAY.
AFTER ALL, WHEN YOU'RE FIGHTING THE BIG BOSS AT THE END OF THE GAME, YOU DON'T JUST SPAM HIM WITH WEBLINES.
YOU HAVE TO FIND HIS WEAKNESS...
...LEARN HIS TIMING...
...AND KNOW WHEN...
...TO MAKE YOUR MOVE.

CHOMP
AAAARRRGH!
BAD IDEA BAD IDEA BAD IDEA
OW OW OW OW OW
I CAN'T EVEN TELL WHAT YOU'RE *TRYING* TO DO, SPIDER-MAN.

OKAY...*CONCENTRATE...* FIGURE THIS OUT...
...THE PROJECTOR'S *INSIDE*, BUT THEN SO'S THE...

THWIP
OH, *YEAH,* OF COURSE.
THERE *IS* ONE WAY TO STOP A VIDEOMAN.
I WAS *RIGHT* ALL ALONG.

YOINK.
WHAK
TAKE AWAY THE BATTERIES...
...AND IT'S GAME OVER.
NOO100--
FXXT
SHOULDA SAVED AT THE LAST CHECKPOINT, FELLA.
AND IT'S JUST AS I SUSPECTED!
A DXS-6502 BATTERY--THE KIND WITH A PARALLEL L TERMINAL, IF I'M NOT--
HEY!
WAP WAP
YOU KILLED PETE!

THWIP
I DIDN'T! HE'S OKAY! I'LL GET HIM!
DON'T GO ANYWHERE!
THE ONLY PLACE I'M GOING IS JAIL--
--TO VISIT YOU! WHEN THEY ARREST YOU FOR KILLING PETE!
YOU LOST THE THREAD, THERE, GANKE.
DIDN'T MARK TWAIN WRITE SOMETHING ABOUT HEARING YOUR OWN EULOGY?
I SHOULD PROBABLY READ SOME CLASSICS-- I'VE DEFINITELY HAD ENOUGH VIDEO GAMES FOR NOW.
I THINK WE ALL HAVE.
GLORIANA GRANT! THIS IS YOUR DOING! I WARNED YOU ABOUT YOUR HOLOGRAM PROJECTOR!
I DIDN'T DO IT.
THERE'S NO WAY MY CODE COULD HAVE CAUSED THIS!
SOMEONE MUST HAVE--
HEY, GUYS...
...I'M OKAY!
SPIDER-MAN SAVED ME! IT WAS PRETTY COOL, ACTUALLY.
SO, NO HARM, NO FOUL.

NO HARM, MR. PARKER? LOOK WHAT GG'S INVENTION DID.
I TOLD YOU, THIS WASN'T A MISTAKE I MADE--IT WAS SABOTAGE.
STOP BLAMING OTHERS FOR YOUR MISTAKES AND PACK YOUR THINGS, GG--YOU'RE GOING HOME.
YOU AND SPIDER-MAN BOTH ALMOST KILLED PARKER.
NOBODY BELIEVES ME ABOUT ANYTHING...
I DO...
...BECAUSE I KNOW VIDEOMAN DIDN'T RUN OFF WITH THE ARC REACTOR.
SOMEBODY WANTED A DISTRACTION-- SO THEY COULD ROB TONY STARK.
PETE! YOU'RE RIGHT!
SPIDER-MAN ISN'T A MURDERER--
--HE'S A THIEF!
OH, NO.
I REALLY, REALLY HAVE TO DO SOMETHING ABOUT MY IMAGE.

3
D.NA
2.18

SPIDER-MAN!
I HAVE YOUR WEB-SPINNING BRACELETS. IF YOU WANT THEM BACK--
--REVEAL YOURSELF!
WELL, WELL, WELL. IF IT ISN'T MY OLD FRIEND, THE BLACK PANTHER.
OR SHOULD I SAY--THE GUY I THOUGHT WAS MY FRIEND. MY SO-CALLED FRIEND. MY FAKE FRIEND.
THERE'S GOT TO BE A WORD FOR THAT...
SPIDER-MAN. DO NOT BE HASTY--

HASTY?! YOU'RE THE ONE BEING HASTY! YOU BELIEVED EVERY BAD THING THEY SAID ABOUT ME--
--AND YOU STOLE MY WEB-SHOOTERS!
SPIDER-MAN-- DON'T!
SPINNING WEBS IS MY THING.
WELL, THAT AND BEING REALLY CHARMING.
BUT CHARM ONLY GETS YOU SO FAR WHEN THE SUPER VILLAINS SHOW UP.
YOU ARE MAKING A MISTAKE, SPIDER-MAN.
WHICH I'M REALLY GOOD AT, AS YOU MAY ALREADY HAVE FIGURED OUT.
SO HERE'S WHERE THE CLICHÉ RECORD SCRATCHES AND I SAY, "YOU'RE PROBABLY ASKING YOURSELF HOW I GOT HERE."
BUT YOU PROBABLY ARE ASKING THAT.

IT STARTED A FEW HOURS AGO, AT STARK CAMP.
SOMETHING'S JUST NOT RIGHT ABOUT THIS.
SALAD'S HEALTHY, GANKE.
YOU KNOW WHAT I MEAN, PETE. SPIDER-MAN FRAMED GG SO HE COULD STEAL THE ARC REACTOR...
...AND I THOUGHT HE WAS ONE OF THE GOOD GUYS.
HE DIDN'T DO EITHER OF THOSE THINGS.
HE IS.
THEN HE TRIED TO HURT YOU.
THAT DOESN'T MATTER, GANKE.
ALL MY PERSONAL PROBLEMS ARE NOTHING.
THE PRESSURE OF COMING UP WITH A FINAL PROJECT...
...THE WORRIES ABOUT FITTING IN WITH THE RICH KIDS AT STARK CAMP...
...NONE OF IT MATTERS WHEN I LOOK AT WHAT'S HAPPENING TO GG.
THIS JUST...THIS ISN'T HER FIGHT.
THIS IS SPIDER-MAN'S PROBLEM.

HOW LONG DO YOU...DO YOU HAVE, GG?
MRS. LIU GAVE ME A STAY OF EXECUTION. I DON'T HAVE TO LEAVE STARK CAMP UNTIL SOME FRIEND OF TONY STARK'S LOOKS INTO MY... SITUATION.

THAT SOUNDS OMINOUS. WHAT FRIEND?
DOESN'T MATTER, RIYA. WHO'S GOING TO BELIEVE SOMEBODY ELSE'S PROGRAMMING MADE MY PROJECT MALFUNCTION?

WELL--THINK THIS THROUGH. THERE HAS TO BE SOME WAY OF PROVING THAT.
UNLESS STARK'S FRIEND CAN LOOK AT LINES OF CODE AND TELL WHO WROTE WHAT, I'M GETTING KICKED OUT OF HERE.

GIVE YOURSELF SOME CREDIT, GG.
IT WOULDN'T TAKE SPIDER-MAN TO MAKE YOUR LITTLE TOY GO HAYWIRE...
...YOU'VE BEEN COMING TO STARK CAMP FOR YEARS AND YOUR STUFF'S ALWAYS WORKED BADLY.

AT LEAST IT'S NOT MY THIRD CELL-PHONE GAME IN A ROW, LACHLAN.

IT'S CALLED "ITERATING"--YOU SHOULD LOOK INTO IT.
CAREFUL, ETHAN, OR SHE'LL SEND HER HOLOGRAM TO BEAT US UP.
COME ON, GG, I'M NOT HUNGRY ANYMORE...

I HOPE I AM NOT INTERRUPTING.
I AM T'CHALLA, KING OF WAKANDA.
TONY STARK ASKED ME TO RESOLVE A PROBLEM AT STARK CAMP. SHALL I BEGIN NOW?
NO PROBLEM HERE, SIR.
GG JUST NEEDED SOME ADVICE ABOUT HER BIG PROJECT...
...BEFORE SHE GOES HOME, I MEAN.
YOU DESIGNED THE AVENGERS' QUINJETS, MR. PANTHER. I ALWAYS WANTED TO ASK--
--WHY'D YOU CALL THEM THAT? IT'S THE ORIGINAL ENGINE ARRANGEMENT, RIGHT? I READ SOMETHING DIFFERENT ON A FRINGO THREAD, BUT I THINK IT WAS THE ENGINES.
AM I RIGHT? CAN I GET YOUR AUTOGRAPH?
THAT...IS A SALAD.
IT'S A REAL HONOR TO MEET YOU.
WINK WINK. PANTHER AND I MET BEFORE, Y'SEE.
I ASSUME STARK TOLD HIM I'M REALLY SPIDER-MAN. HE MUST BE HERE TO CLEAR MY NAME.

I MEAN, WHY ELSE WOULD STARK CALL IN THE *BLACK PANTHER?*
ER...
THE *DORA MILAJE* ARE ZEALOUS BODYGUARDS, AND I AM *THANKFUL* FOR THEM.
BUT I DON'T THINK THIS *TEENAGE BOY* IS A THREAT.
ARE YOU THE ONE WHO WAS *TOSSED AWAY* BY SPIDER-MAN YESTERDAY?
WELL, I WOULDN'T SAY *"TOSSED"* EXACTLY...

PANTHER'S HERE TO *CLEAR* SPIDER-MAN'S NAME.
THAT'S REAL LUCKY--I HAD A NEW *KILLBLAST TRIGGER* AD BUILT WITH SPIDEY, BUT *GRABBIT* HAS RULES ABOUT *MONETIZING CRIMINALS.*

TONY STARK HIMSELF COULD NOT BE HERE DUE TO AN INCIDENT IN *SYMKARIA* REQUIRING HIS ATTENTION.
AS I WAS IN NEW YORK, ADDRESSING THE UNITED NATIONS, HE HAS ASKED *ME* TO DETERMINE IF SPIDER-MAN HAS *INDEED* ENDANGERED YOU...
...AND IF HE HAS *TRULY* STOLEN AN *ARC REACTOR.* THIS IS A MATTER OF NO SMALL CONCERN--IN THE WRONG HANDS, EVEN A *SMALL* ARC REACTOR IS AN INTERNATIONAL THREAT.

SO I MUST ASK THAT YOU TELL ME EVERYTHING YOU KNOW ABOUT *SPIDER-MAN...*

"...AFTER THE DORA MILAJE AND I INVESTIGATE THE GROUNDS."
DO YOU THINK HE'LL FIND ANY WEBS?
WHAT?
WELL, I FIGURE BLACK PANTHER CAN FIND CLUES BETTER THAN US.
ENOUGH OF THIS, GANKE.
WHAT?
I'M SICK OF YOU TRASHING SPIDER-MAN.
PETE! HE ALMOST KILLED YOU!
HE SAVED ME!
WHAT WAS HE EVEN DOING HERE, THEN? I MEAN, ONE TIME, I GET.
HE WAS PROBABLY LOOKING OUT FOR US AS A FAVOR FOR STARK.
THEN WHY IS PANTHER HERE? SEE? IT DOESN'T MAKE ANY SENSE!
GANKE'S GOT A POINT. IT'S GETTING HARDER TO MAKE UP EXCUSES FOR SPIDER-MAN SHOWING UP.
TAKE THESE METAL DETECTORS--NEW, POST BREAK-IN NUMBER TWO.
THEY KEEP TRACK OF WHAT'S GOING IN AND OUT...WHICH INCLUDES, BY DESIGN OR CHANCE, MY WEB-SHOOTERS.
SO, YEAH, GANKE'S GOT A POINT...

...BUT THAT DOESN'T MAKE HIS CONSTANT ANTI-SPIDEY-NESS ANY LESS IRRITATING.
I CAN'T BELIEVE I EVER LIKED HIM.
ALSO, I CAN'T BELIEVE I AGREE WITH THAT DAILY BUGLE GUY ABOUT ANYTHING...
OKAY, GANKE, OKAY... HEY. YOU SEEN MY SUITCASE?
YOUR CIRCUIT BOARDS HAVE A WAY OF... SPREADING OUT.
THERE'S MORE IMPORTANT THINGS TO WORRY ABOUT THAN YOUR SUITCASE, PETE.
NOT ONLY DO WE HAVE GG IN TROUBLE AND SPIDER-MAN TURNING BAD--
--WE STILL NEED TO FIGURE OUT YOUR PROJECT. THE CLOCK'S TICKING.
I KNOW WHAT THE CLOCK IS DOING--I JUST WANT MY SUITCASE!
ALL RIGHT, HANG ON--IT CAN'T HAVE GONE FAR.
YOU KNOW WHAT--FORGET IT.
I DON'T NEED A SUITCASE. I NEED SOME AIR. I'LL BE BACK.
HEY, PETE--

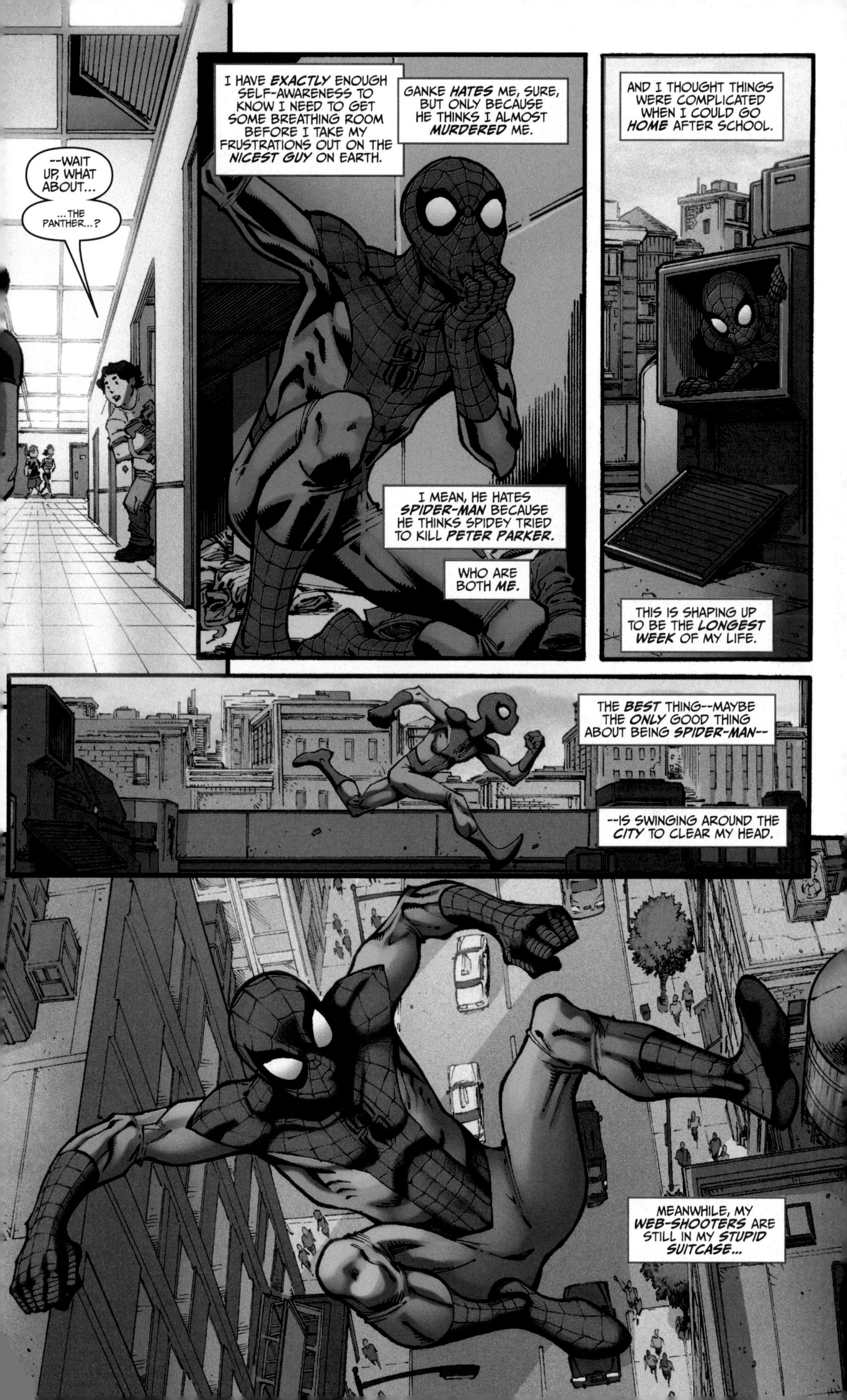
--WAIT UP, WHAT ABOUT...
...THE PANTHER...?
I HAVE EXACTLY ENOUGH SELF-AWARENESS TO KNOW I NEED TO GET SOME BREATHING ROOM BEFORE I TAKE MY FRUSTRATIONS OUT ON THE NICEST GUY ON EARTH.
GANKE HATES ME, SURE, BUT ONLY BECAUSE HE THINKS I ALMOST MURDERED ME.
I MEAN, HE HATES SPIDER-MAN BECAUSE HE THINKS SPIDEY TRIED TO KILL PETER PARKER.
WHO ARE BOTH ME.
AND I THOUGHT THINGS WERE COMPLICATED WHEN I COULD GO HOME AFTER SCHOOL.
THIS IS SHAPING UP TO BE THE LONGEST WEEK OF MY LIFE.
THE BEST THING--MAYBE THE ONLY GOOD THING ABOUT BEING SPIDER-MAN--
--IS SWINGING AROUND THE CITY TO CLEAR MY HEAD.
MEANWHILE, MY WEB-SHOOTERS ARE STILL IN MY STUPID SUITCASE...

...AND WHO KNOWS WHERE GANKE PUT THAT.
MY EXPERTISE IS GENETICS, NOT COMPUTERS--
--SO DON'T TAKE THIS AS MISTRUST, BUT I HAVE NO IDEA WHAT YOU'RE SAYING, GG.
I KNOW. THAT'S THE PROBLEM. MRS. LIU IS A PHYSICIST. SHE DOESN'T KNOW ABOUT...ABOUT VIDEO GAMES.
SHE PROBABLY THINKS THIS IS A WASTE OF TIME, COMPARED TO WEIGHING THE SUN OR WHATEVER.
I DON'T THINK IT'S A WASTE OF TIME.
MAYBE I CAN HELP.
IF YOU WANT.
PETE RAN OFF, AND I WAS JUST SITTING THERE AND...
PARKER'S PROBABLY TRYING TO FIGURE OUT WHAT PLUG TO PULL OR WHATEVER.
HE STRIKES ME AS THE KIND OF GUY WHO ISN'T INTERESTED IF HE'S NOT THE MAIN CHARACTER.

I DON'T THINK THAT'S TRUE.
HE, UH, GOT MAD AT ME BECAUSE HE COULDN'T FIND A SUITCASE.
THEN WHY'D HE RUN OFF?
OH, THAT SOUNDS REASONABLE.
HEY. THIS CODE IS DIFFERENT.
YOU CAN TELL?
YEAH, OF COURSE. IT'S NOT SLOPPY, EXACTLY, IT'S JUST--
THE REST IS MORE EFFICIENT.
RIGHT, LIKE WHOEVER WROTE IT KNEW WHAT YOUR HOLOGRAM THING DID, BUT NOT EXACTLY HOW YOU'D DONE IT.
I'M GOING TO TRY TO FIND MRS. LIU.
SHE NEEDS TO HEAR THIII--WAHH!
HEADS UP, RIYA. I DON'T KNOW WHY OU LEFT THAT RATTY OLD SUITCASE OUT ANYWAY.
ME? I THOUGHT YOU--
DID YOU SAY "SUITCASE"?
SOMETHING REAL WEIRD IS GOING ON HERE, GUYS.
WE GOTTA FIND PETE.

I'LL BE RIGHT BACK, I JUST FEEL LIKE THIS IS TOO SUSPICIOUS TO--
SUSPICIOUS?
PERHAPS I SHOULD BE THE JUDGE OF THAT.
UH. IT'S MY ROOMMATE'S.
PETE MUST HAVE LEFT IT HERE.
AND WHAT WAS THE ELUSIVE MR. PARKER DOING IN THE ROOM OF MISS GRANT AND MISS CHAMBAL?
UH. HELPING GG PROVE SHE DIDN'T WRECK THE LABORATORY. I, UH, BET.
I MEAN, I KNOW SHE'S NOT RESPONSIBLE FOR DESTROYING STUFF!
HEY! YOU CAN'T!
TELL YOUR ROOMMATE TO FIND ME, AND I'LL HAPPILY RETURN IT.
IN THE MEANTIME, MR. LEE...

"...PLEASE KEEP AN EYE OUT FOR ANYTHING UNUSUAL."
I KNOW WHAT YOU'RE THINKING: NITRATES.
BUT SOMETIMES YOU JUST REALLY NEED COMFORT FOOD.
SIGH
SOUND OF NO WEB BEING THWIPPED.
WELL, AT LEAST WE HAVE EACH OTHER, HOT DOG.
SPIDER-MAN!
OH, GOOD, SOUNDS LIKE SOMEBODY ELSE IS MAD AT ME.
CAN'T WAIT TO FIND OUT WHO.
I HAVE YOUR WEB-SPINNING BRACELETS. IF YOU WANT THEM BACK...
WELL, THAT'S GOOD NEWS.
I ALREADY KNEW BLACK PANTHER WAS MAD AT ME.
THIS IS MY LUCKY DAY.

ANNNNND THIS IS WHERE WE CAME IN.
ME TRYING TO THINK OF A SINGLE WORD THAT SUMS UP "I THOUGHT PANTHER AND I WERE FRIENDS, AND HERE WE ARE, FIGHTING ON A ROOFTOP."
WELL, TRYING TO FIGHT, ANYWAY.
BLACK PANTHER HAS, AMONG OTHER ABILITIES, A PERFECT KINESTHETIC SENSE.
THAT MEANS HE KNOWS EXACTLY WHERE EVERY BODY PART IS, AT EVERY INSTANT.
AND CAN PRECISELY CONTROL THOSE FEET, FISTS, AND CLAWS.
MEANWHILE, I HAVE MY PATENTED SPIDER-SENSE, WHICH WARNS ME WHEN I'M IN DANGER.

WE COULD LITERALLY BE DOING THIS ALL DAY.
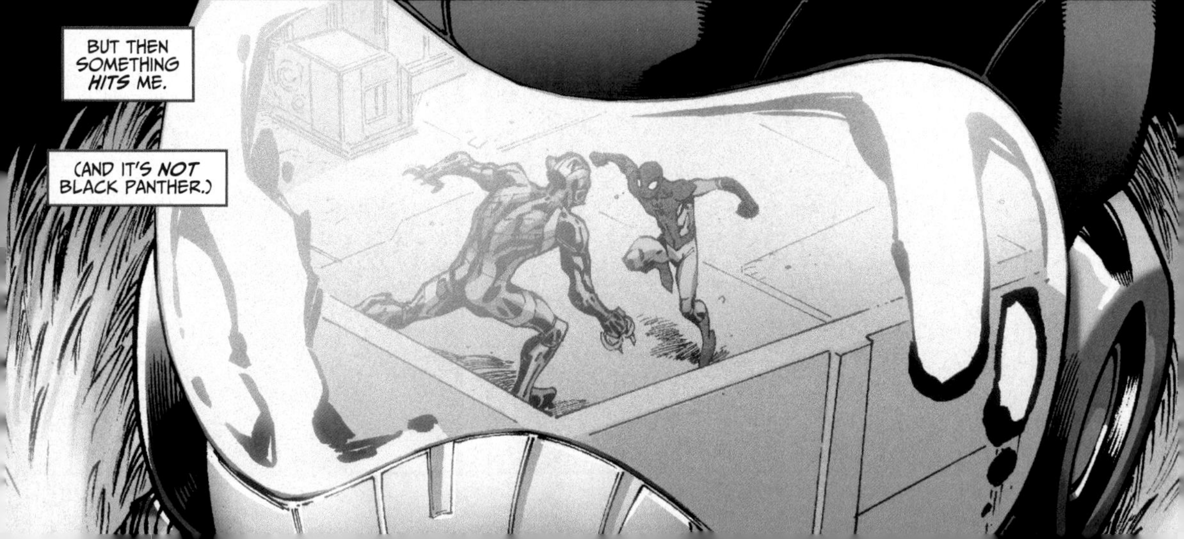
BUT THEN SOMETHING HITS ME.
(AND IT'S NOT BLACK PANTHER.)

IT'S THE REALIZATION THAT WHILE WE'RE BOTH STAYING ONE STEP AHEAD OF EACH OTHER, MY SPIDER-SENSE SHOULD BE BUZZING LIKE A HORNETS' NEST--
(TO MIX ARTHROPOD METAPHORS.)
BUT MY SPIDER-SENSE IS TOTALLY SILENT.
WHICH IS WEIRD, WHAT WITH THE DEADLY CLAWS AND ALL.
YOU CAN GET HIM, SPIDEY!
WE BELIEVE IN YOU! AND IN THE SALES YOU'LL GENERATE FOR OUR MOBILE APP!
LIFESTYLE.
I MEAN OUR MOBILE LIFESTYLE!
HANG ON--IF THESE YO-YOS ARE ROOTING FOR ME...
...AND YOU'RE NOT ACTUALLY TRYING TO HURT ME...
...AM I THE BAD GUY HERE?
WHAT DO YOU THINK I AM TRYING TO TELL YOU?!
I BELIEVED US TO BE FRIENDS!

UH, YEAH.
I WAS CALLING YOU SO I COULD RETURN THESE TO YOU.
I, UH...MAYBE THIS ONE'S ON ME. I MIGHT HAVE MISINTERPRETED EVENTS.
AW, COME ON.
NOBODY WANTS TO WATCH A VIDEO OF HEROES BEING NICE.
FIGHT EACH OTHER!
YOU KNOW THOSE TWO?
NO, NOPE, NOT AT ALL.
WHY'D YOU TAKE MY WEB-SHOOTERS IF WE'RE ON THE SAME SIDE?

THEY WERE PLANTED IN GLORIANA GRANT'S ROOM, IN A SUITCASE BELONGING TO ONE PETER PARKER.
MR. PARKER'S ROOMMATE LOCATED THE SUITCASE. HE DOES NOT KNOW WHAT WAS INSIDE... BUT HE SEEMED CONCERNED.

I BELIEVE HE MAY BE A GOOD FRIEND.
NICEST GUY ON EARTH.
WE SHOULD VALUE OUR FRIENDS, AND AID THEM, AS WHEN TONY STARK TOLD ME OUR MUTUAL FRIEND SPIDER-MAN SEEMED TO BE IN TROUBLE...

YEAH.
SOMEONE APPEARS TO HAVE UNCOVERED YOUR SECRET IDENTITY. AND I AM AFRAID THAT MEANS THE FRIENDS OF PETER PARKER...

"...MAY FIND THEMSELVES PULLED INTO THE WORLD OF SPIDER-MAN."
RIGHT THERE, THAT THIRD BLOCK OF CODE.
YEAH, I ALMOST MISSED IT. OKAY, THAT ONE IS SLOPPY.
THEY HAD TO ASSUME I WAS USING A MASS-DISTORT TRANSCRIPTION AND A--
AHEM.
I THOUGHT, MAYBE, WE COULD TEAM UP.
OR SOMETHING.
AND SINCE I DON'T KNOW THE FIRST THING ABOUT WRITING VIDEO GAMES...
...WELL, I BROUGHT DRINKS.
IN PLASTIC BOTTLES. PARKER, YOU'RE KILLING THE PLANET.
THERE'S ANOTHER BADLY WRITTEN LINE. MRS. LIU IS GONNA HAVE TO BELIEVE YOU DIDN'T DO THIS.
GLORIANA...I'M SORRY THAT YOU GOT--
GG.
WHAT?
THE NAME'S GG.
HEY, PETE. YOU GOT A SECOND?
I SHOULDN'T HAVE SNAPPED AT YOU EARLIER.
YEAH, YEAH, I KNOW. BUT SOMETHING REAL WEIRD HAPPENED. SOMEBODY STOLE YOUR SUITCASE AND--

AND NOW BLACK PANTHER RETURNS IT, NO WORSE FOR THE WEAR.
KING T'CHALLA ALSO STRAIGHTENED OUT THE ISSUE REGARDING SPIDER-MAN--
--AND HE CONCURRED WITH RIYA THAT I SHOULD TAKE ANOTHER LOOK AT MISS GRANT'S CODE...
THE BLACK PANTHER PROBABLY KNOWS ENOUGH ABOUT COMPUTERS TO TELL WHAT I WROTE AND DIDN'T.
I GUESS THE SUITCASE MIGHT'VE JUST BEEN A WEIRD HOUSEKEEPING THING. I GUESS.
THAT MUST BE IT. LOOK, I REALLY APPRECIATE YOU--
LA LI LA LI DE DA
HANG ON, THAT'S MY PHONE.
OH, BOY. I'VE BEEN HERE THREE DAYS, SURVIVED TWO ROBBERIES, A MALEVOLENT VIDEO GAME AVATAR, AND A FIGHT WITH THE BLACK PANTHER...
...AND I HAVEN'T CALLED MY AUNT.
SHE'S GONNA BE THE ONE WHO KILLS ME.
AUNT MAY! SORRY I DIDN'T CALL. I JUST GOT CARRIED AWAY OVER HERE.
DID I MISS ANYTHING BIG?

YOU COULD SAY THAT.

4

WE'VE GOT YOUR AUNT.
DON'T TELL ANYBODY OR YOU'LL NEVER SEE HER AGAIN.
CLICK
Aunt May
Call ended
0:0:14
THIS SEEMS AN INEFFICIENT WAY TO DISTRIBUTE WATER.
YEAH, WELL...
SEE THIS? I DIDN'T WRITE THAT CODE.
AUNT MAY.
I THINK YOU'D HAVE TO GO LINE BY LINE AND COMPARE, BUT MAYBE...
...MAYBE...
PARKER? YOU OKAY?
I...
...MY...
...I...
...HAVE TO...
...GO...
WONDER WHAT'S UP WITH PETE?

WHERE YOU RUNNIN' TO NOW, PARKER?
YOU SEE YOUR SHADOW AND THINK IT'S ANOTHER SUPER VILLAIN?
HELLO-- POLICE? THERE'S BEEN A BREAK-IN--
--AND I THINK SOMEBODY ATTACKED MY AUNT.
NO, I'M NOT THERE. I'M NOT EVEN CLOSE.
UNFORTUNATELY.
SOMEBODY ATTACKED AUNT MAY.
THAT MEANS THEY KNOW I'M SPIDER-MAN AND THEY WENT AFTER MY FAMILY.
BUT WHO-- WHY--HOW?!
FOCUS, PARKER. THOSE QUESTIONS ARE FOR LATER. RIGHT NOW--

--GETTING TO MAY IS ALL THAT MATTERS.
THEY SAID NOT TO TELL ANYBODY, BUT COME ON. STILL--ASSUMING THESE ARE SUPER VILLAINS, THE COPS MIGHT BE HELPLESS.
THE STARK SCIENCE CENTER IS IN WASHINGTON HEIGHTS--ABOUT FOURTEEN MILES FROM HOME.
IF I HAD A QUINJET, I'D BE IN FOREST HILLS IN SECONDS.
BUT I'M NOT AN AVENGER.
I'M JUST ME.
AND MY AUNT NEEDS ME.
(I WAS JUST IN A FIGHT WITH THE BLACK PANTHER!)
SO ALL I CAN DO IS CUT EAST AND FOLLOW THE HARLEM RIVER.
(YESTERDAY I FOUGHT A HOLOGRAM!)
OVER RANDALL'S ISLAND, THROUGH ASTORIA.
(MY ARM WANTS TO COME OUT OF ITS SOCKET.)
PUSH. SWING. JUMP.
(I WANT TO SLEEP!)
PAST MIDTOWN HIGH.
AUNT
MAY
NEEDS
ME!

AND ME...?
I NEEDED SOME GOOD NEWS.
INSTEAD, I GET RUBBLE.
SHE'S GONE.
MY AUNT'S GONE AND THERE'S NOTHING I CAN...
...NO.
THERE'S NOT JUST RUBBLE.
THERE'S A TRAIL.
I'VE GOT TO KEEP MOVING. DOESN'T MATTER HOW EXHAUSTED I AM.
DOESN'T MATTER THAT THERE AREN'T ANY TALL BUILDINGS.
POLICE LINE
DO NOT CROSS
POLICE LINE

IF I USE MY MOMENTUM...
...I CAN STAY SWINGING...
...BUT ONLY IF I MOVE FAST ENOUGH.
GOOD THING AUNT MAY NEEDS ME TO GO FAST.
THEY CAN'T HAVE MADE IT FAR.
NYPD
NYPD
OR CAN THEY? WHAT IF THE ATTACKERS HAVE SUPER-SPEED?
OR THEY CAN TELEPORT?
WHAT IF THEY BURROWED UNDERGROUND?
OH, I KNOW THIS GUY. HE'S GOT MY SPIDER-SENSE TINGLING LIKE CRAZY.
AUNT MAY'S NOT MOVING. SHE... SHE MIGHT BE...
NO.
IT DOESN'T MEAN ANYTHING. SHE'S JUST UNCONSCIOUS. SHE HAS TO BE.

HEY, RHINO-- WHY DON'T YOU PICK ON SOMEBODY YOUR OWN--
ZZZAPPPP
SPIDER-MAN...?
OKAY...I GUESS THAT'S WHY MY SPIDEY-SENSE WAS GOING OFF.
I SHOULD'VE KNOWN.
THAT BLAST WAS FROM THE VOICE ON THE PHONE...
...THE SHOCKER.
HE TRIED TO ROB THE STARK CENTER A COUPLE DAYS AGO.
BUT HOW DID HE FIGURE OUT MY IDENTITY?
SPIDER-MAN?! WHAT AN UNEXPECTED BONUS!

SARCASM ISN'T YOUR STRONG SUIT, SHOCKER.
LET HER GO AND WE CAN TALK THIS OUT WITH OUR FISTS LIKE REASONABLE SUPER-PEOPLE.
YOU KIDDING? I'VE BEEN ITCHING FOR A REMATCH.
NOBODY'S GONNA USE HOLOGRAMS TO SAVE YOU NOW.
OKAY. IT'S ALL MAKING SENSE.
SHOCKER TRIED TO STEAL STUFF. GG STOPPED HIM WITH HER BRICK-WALL PROJECTOR.
SO SHOCKER...REPROGRAMMED THE PROJECTOR TO FIGHT ME WHILE HE STOLE A MINI ARC REACTOR...?
BUT WHY GO AFTER MAY? WHERE'S THE REACTOR?
AND HOW DOES HE KNOW PETER PARKER IS SPIDER-MAN?!
YOU GOT LUCKY SOMEBODY PUT A BRICK WALL BETWEEN US--OR I'D'VE DONE THIS SOONER.
TOUGH TALK.

LET--
--HER--
--GO!
ERP!
RHINO, OL' BUDDY--
--I COULD USE SOME HELP HERE!
POW
HUHH... HUHH...
EVERY PART OF ME HURTS.
I WANT TO FALL INTO A LITTLE SPIDER-HEAP.
THANKS FOR THE ASSIST, SPIDER-MAN.
YOU... YOU OKAY?
I BETTER BE.

HEY-- SHOCKER?
WHERE'D YOU--
OH. I GET IT.
THERE'S A FIRST.
SAYYY... THAT GRAY OUTFIT MAKES YOU INCONSPICUOUS AS ALL GET-OUT--BUT DON'T I REMEMBER YOU FROM SOMEWHERE?
DIDN'T YOU TRY TO ROB A BANK OR SOMETHING?
GRAHHH!
NOBODY FORGETS THE RHINO!
UNNHHH... WHO...?
SHE'S AWAKE! SHE'S OKAY!
OR AS OKAY AS YOU CAN BE WHEN YOU'RE IN THE CLUTCHES OF A DOOFUS IN A RHINO OUTFIT.
MAY!

"MAY" WHAT?
MAY GO FLYING AFTER I POUND YOU?
WHAM
UNNF!
AND HERE I HEARD HIPPOS WERE THE MOST DANGEROUS ANIMAL.
I'LL SHOW YOU DANGEROUS!
LET GO OF ME YOU-- YOU--
--WHATEVER YOU ARE!
I THINK HE'S SUPPOSED TO BE A DINOSAUR.
PROBABLY HASN'T HEARD THEY HAD FEATHERS.
YOU KNOW I'M THE RHINO!
YOU JUST SAID SO!
YOU'RE PAYING MORE ATTENTION THAN I WAS GIVING YOU CREDIT FOR...
NYPD

WHA--?!
...BUT TO BE FAIR, I WAS NOT GIVING YOU MUCH CREDIT.
NOTHING STOPS THE RHINO!
SORRY, HORN-HEAD. THAT'S SOMEBODY ELSE'S CATCH-PHRASE.
GOTTA GET YOUR OWN.
I KNEW THIS WAS A BAD IDEA!
NEVER SHOULDA LISTENED TO SHOCKER.
WAIT-- DON'T--
AAAHHH--

HUNFF!
RELAX, MAY--
--UH--
--MAY'AM. I GOT THIS HANDLED.
HEY, RHINO!
MAYBE NOTHING STOPS YOU BECAUSE YOU DON'T KNOW WHEN TO QUIT!
THERE WEREN'T SUPPOSED TO BE ANY SUPER HEROES ON THIS JOB.
THE COPS SHOULDN'TA BEEN THAT FAST.
NOBODY WAS SUPPOSED TO GET--
--HURT.

THWAMM
YEEE-OWWWW!
MY HAND!!! WHAT ARE YOU MADE OF?!
TOUGHER STUFF THAN YOU, KID.
HAHAHA--
HARGHK--!
CAHHN'T-- REAHHTHE--
HE CAN BREATHE. I BLOCKED UP HIS MOUTH, NOT HIS AIRWAY.
BUT WHEN YOU'RE NOT EXPECTING THAT--IT SURE DOES FEEL LIKE YOU CAN'T BREATHE...

...WHICH MAKES YOU PANIC--
--AND THAT PUTS YOU IN A VULNERABLE POSITION, NO MATTER WHAT KIND OF ARMOR YOU HAVE GRAFTED ONTO YOUR SKIN.
I LAY THE WEBS ON AS THICK AS I CAN.
IT WON'T HOLD RHINO FOREVER, BUT I DON'T NEED FOREVER--
--I JUST NEED LONG ENOUGH TO MAKE SURE AUNT MAY'S OKAY.
SPIDEY--YOU GOT HIM.
THE PRECINCT JUST RADIOED--AN AVENGERS TEAM IS ON ITS WAY.
YOU DID IT.
UHHHH.
STOPPED HIM. BOTH OF THEM.
SO TIRED. SO HURT.
MAY!

ARE--ARE YOU OKAY?
THIS WASN'T SUPPOSED TO HAPPEN.
NO, I KNOW, I--
I'M A NORMAL PERSON! I WAS GOING TO WORK!
HOW DID I GET PUT IN YOUR STORY?
WHAT WOULD HAVE HAPPENED IF MY NEPHEW HAD BEEN HERE...?
ARE WE SUPPOSED TO LIVE IN A WORLD WHERE THIS JUST HAPPENS TO PEOPLE?!
I--I DON'T KNOW.
I...
YOU GOT KNOCKED OUT. THAT'S REALLY DANGEROUS.
SO MAKE SURE THE EMTs TAKE A GOOD LOOK AT YOU, OKAY? PROMISE ME.
I...I WILL.
THANKS. I GOTTA GO BEFORE THE COPS DECIDE TO ARREST ME.
SPIDEY-- WAIT!
I'M NOT GONNA PUSH THE PARKER LUCK.

BUT I'M *ALSO* NOT ABOUT TO WEB-SWING ALL THE WAY BACK TO THE *STARK CENTER.*
I GRABBED SOME *CLOTHES* FROM MY *HOUSE*--WHICH WAS *REALLY EASY,* WHAT WITH THE *GIANT HOLE.*
I DIDN'T THINK I'D BE ABLE TO KEEP MY *EYELIDS* OPEN ON THE *A TRAIN...*
...BUT MY *MIND* WOULDN'T LET ME SLEEP.
WHY WERE SHOCKER AND RHINO PLAYING *DUMB* ABOUT KNOWING WHO I AM?
MARIA STARK SCIENCE CENTER
ARE THEY GONNA SPILL THE BEANS TO THE *COPS?*
IF MY IDENTITY GETS OUT... I MEAN, WHAT HAPPENED TO *AUNT MAY*--THAT'S *WHY* I HAVE A SECRET IDENTITY.
MR. PARKER!
HEY, KING T'CHALLA.
I WAS WORRIED WHEN YOU DID NOT *RETURN.*
BY THE TIME I FIGURED OUT WHERE YOU HAD *GONE,* YOU HAD TAKEN CARE OF THE VILLAINS.
I DIDN'T HAVE A CHOICE.
MR. PARKER-- DO NOT MAKE THE SAME MISTAKE YOU MADE THIS AFTERNOON. YOU ARE NOT *ALONE.*
WE COULD HAVE *TEAMED UP.*
NEXT TIME. FIRST, I GOTTA SLEEP.

UGH. WAS I JUST RUDE TO THE BLACK PANTHER?
I'M TOO TIRED TO DO ANYTHING ABOUT IT. ANYWAY--
--WHAT "NEXT TIME"?
PETE! YOU LOOK TERRIBLE!
I SAW ON FRINGO HOW RHINO AND ELECTRO ATTACKED SOME LADY. KING T'CHALLA SAID SHE WAS YOUR AUNT.
SHE IS. AND IT WAS SHOCKER, NOT ELECTRO.
MY AUNT-- SHE CALLED ME. I TRIED TO GET HOME...BUT I GOT BEATEN UP...
OH. SOMEBODY PUT UP FOOTAGE OF SPIDER-MAN. IT LOOKED LIKE HE DID A GOOD JOB PROTECTING YOUR AUNT.
SO YOU DON'T THINK HE'S A KILLER OR ROBBER ANYMORE?
I'M PRETTY SURE HE'S A HERO. YOU KNOW--IF YOU'RE STILL LOOKING FOR A FINAL PROJECT IDEA--

I'M NOT. I'M DONE WITH STARK CAMP. I'M GOING TO HELP MY AUNT, FIRST THING IN THE MORNING.
OR AFTERNOON. WHENEVER I WAKE--
WHOA!
EARTHQUAKE?
THE WAY THIS WEEK'S BEEN GOING--

"--THIS IS PROBABLY SOMETHING WAY WORSE."
I DO NOT THINK TONY STARK INVITED YOU HERE.
NO...I WOULDN'T SAY HE DID. I WASN'T EXPECTING TO FIND ANY AVENGERS HANGING AROUND HERE.
I HEARD YOU WERE BUSY IN FOREST HILLS.
THEN IT LOOKS AS THOUGH THIS IS YOUR LUCKY DAY.
OKOYE, XOLISWA--MAKE SURE THE CHILDREN ARE SAFE!
AS YOU SAY, MY KING.
BUT OUR JOB IS TO--
XOLISWA! THE KING IS CORRECT--

"--THE SAFETY OF OTHERS IS PARAMOUNT!"
SOMEBODY'S BREAKING IN! AGAIN!
GREEN OUTFIT. FLIES. BUT NOT THE GOBLIN, IT'S THE OTHER GUY.
VULTURE. MAKES SENSE. HE'S WORKED WITH SHOCKER BEFORE...
...NOT THAT I CAN LET GANKE KNOW I KNOW THAT.
UH, LOOK. THAT, UH...
...THAT REMINDS ME. I HAVE TO... UM...

PETE.
GO BE SPIDER-MAN.

WHAAAAT?!
NO, I MEAN, I--

WE'LL TALK ABOUT IT LATER.
I KNOW YOU'RE TIRED, PETE. AND I'VE ONLY KNOWN YOU A COUPLE DAYS. BUT YOU REMIND ME OF A FRIEND OF MINE. I CAN TELL...

..YOU'RE NOT ONNA SLEEP EN SOMEBODY EEDS HELP."
THE SKY IS MY DOMAIN!
I DO NOT THINK YOU UNDERSTAND WHO YOU FACE.
SKRASSH
BUT I SURE DO.
HEY, VULTURE. HOW YOU BEEN?
AND BLACK PANTHER...
...YOU STILL INTERESTED IN A TEAM-UP?

5

SKRACH
NO, NO-- OVER THERE! HE'S GOING AROUND!
I CAN SEE THAT! JUST STAY OUT OF MY--
FZZAAPP
OOPS. SORRY!
IT'S BEEN A LONG WEEK, AND IT'S NOT EVEN CLOSE TO FRIDAY.
I WAS LOOKING FORWARD TO JUST BEING PETER PARKER--LEARNING ABOUT SCIENCE AND TECHNOLOGY AT STARK CAMP.
THEN SOME SUPER VILLAINS FIGURED OUT MY IDENTITY AND WENT AFTER AUNT MAY.
FOLLOW MY LEAD AND FLANK HIM!
THAT MEANS THE BACK, RIGHT, PANTHER?
NOW THEY KEEP TRYING TO ROB THIS PLACE.
ON THE POSITIVE SIDE, BLACK PANTHER AND I FINALLY TEAMED UP.
WHERE ON EARTH DID YOU TRAIN, SPIDER-MAN?
THE MEAN STREETS OF FOREST HILLS, MOSTLY...
SMASH
SIGH.
TOLDYA IT'S BEEN A LONG WEEK.

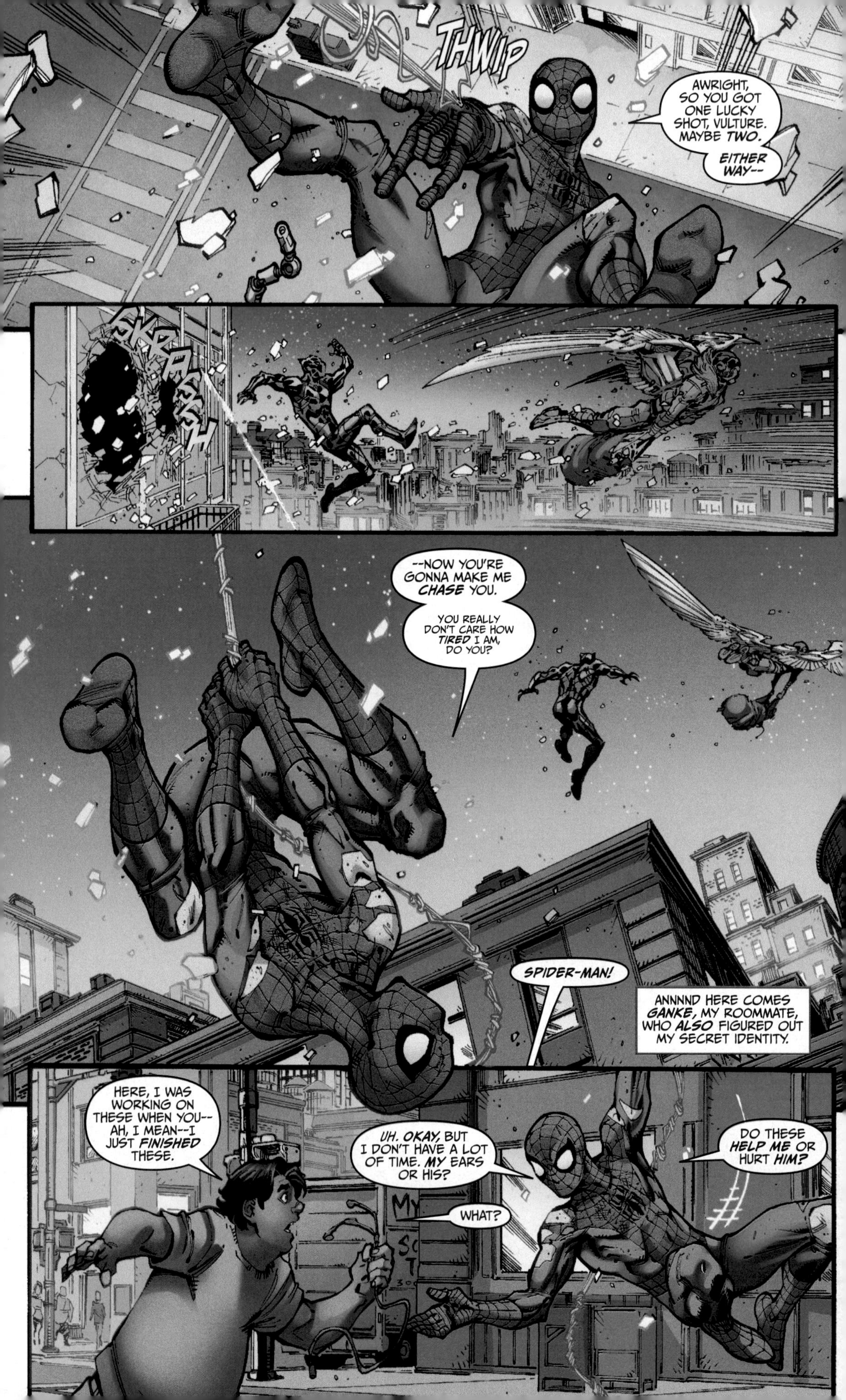
THWIP
AWRIGHT, SO YOU GOT ONE LUCKY SHOT, VULTURE. MAYBE TWO.
EITHER WAY--
SKRASSH
--NOW YOU'RE GONNA MAKE ME CHASE YOU.
YOU REALLY DON'T CARE HOW TIRED I AM, DO YOU?
SPIDER-MAN!
ANNNND HERE COMES GANKE, MY ROOMMATE, WHO ALSO FIGURED OUT MY SECRET IDENTITY.
HERE, I WAS WORKING ON THESE WHEN YOU-- AH, I MEAN--I JUST FINISHED THESE.
UH. OKAY, BUT I DON'T HAVE A LOT OF TIME. MY EARS OR HIS?
WHAT?
DO THESE HELP ME OR HURT HIM?

YOU! HELP! HELP YOU IS WHAT THEY--
WAIT! YOU DIDN'T LET ME TELL YOU WHAT I'M GOING TO DO!
BAD GUY'S GETTING AWAY! WE'LL FIGURE THIS OUT AS WE GO!
GANKE LEE-- GET IN HERE BEFORE YOU GET KILLED!
THIS IS SERIOUS BUSINESS.
YES, MRS. LIU. SORRY, MRS. LIU. I JUST SAW SPIDER-MAN AND GOT EXCITED.
I THOUGHT YOU HATED SPIDER-MAN.
THINGS CHANGE.
THE VULTURE'S GOT A HEAD START, AND SPIDEY NEEDS OUR HELP.
SCIENCE
HA HA HA!
YOU GONNA PULL ON SOME TIGHTS AND A CAPE?
I'VE GOT SOMETHING BETTER THAN A CAPE.
WHAT?
MY PHONE.
I CAN SEE THAT. I DIDN'T MEAN "WHAT'S BETTER THAN A CAPE?" ALMOST EVERYTHING IS.
I MEAN, WHAT ARE YOU PLANNING?
NEW YORK IS THE CITY THAT NEVER SLEEPS, GG...

"...AND THAT MEANS SOMEBODY'S ALWAYS WATCHING."
WE LOST HIM?
OUR QUARRY CAN FLY, SPIDER-MAN. HE KNOWS HOW TO USE THIS CITY AGAINST US. BUT HE HAS NO IDEA WHAT WE TOGETHER CAN--
WE LOST HIM.
ONLY FOR A MOMENT.
DAILY BUGLE
REPORTING ON THE THREATS AND MENACES YOU ABOUT SU
WHAT IS THAT SOUND?
UH, HANG ON. I GUESS I'M GETTING A CALL.
PARDON ME FOR A SEC...
YOU HAVE NO NEED TO TURN AROUND. I KNOW WHO YOU ARE.
YEAH, SORRY, FORCE OF HABIT.
WHAT IS IT?
SPIDER-MAN? THIS IS GANKE, YOU KNOW, FROM THE STARK CAMP.
YOU GAVE ME THE HEADPHONES. I KNOW WHO YOU ARE.
OH, YEAH, RIGHT. BECAUSE I GAVE YOU THE HEADPHONES, THAT'S WHAT YOU KNOW ME FROM. ER, I'M NOT ALONE HERE.
I GATHERED.
IT'S, UH, THAT GIRL WHO MADE THAT HOLOGRAM THAT TRIED TO KILL YOU.
NOT ON PURPOSE.
WHAT DO YOU WANT, GANKE?
I KNOW WHERE THE VULTURE IS.
SOMEBODY JUST POSTED A PIC ON FRINGO.

THE POPULAR SOCIAL MEDIA APP THAT I DIDN'T JUST LEARN ABOUT?
THE PIC'S FROM THE CORNER OF 157TH AND BROADWAY.
WE'RE ON OUR WAY!
AND YET...
GANKE-- VULTURE'S NOT HERE.
YEAH, I KNOW--IT TAKES A FEW SECONDS TO POST A PIC.
SO YOU FIGURED OUT A COMPLICATED WAY TO SEE WHERE HE WAS. GREAT.
YOU HEAR THAT? GG'S WRITING AN ALGORITHM TO TRACK ALL THE SIGHTINGS.
WE'RE WORKING ON IT!
WOW. A REALLY CLEANLY CODED ALGORITHM.
IT'S NO DIFFERENT THAN WRITING DROP RATES IN A GAME. JUST, YOU KNOW, BACKWARDS.
WITH ENOUGH DATA POINTS, SOME KIND OF CONCLUSION SHOULD PRESENT ITSELF.
GOOD THING LUCK HASN'T LET ME DOWN YET.
GIVE IT A MINUTE--WE HAVE ST. NICHOLAS AND 160TH. ALSO EDGECOMBE AND 157TH.
THOSE ARE IN OPPOSITE DIRECTIONS, GANKE.
VULTURE'S GETTING AWAY. I'M JUST GOING TO PICK ONE AND GO FOR IT.
NOW'S NOT THE TIME TO TRUST THE FORCE, SPIDEY!
GG'S SYNCING THE DATA CROSS-PLATFORM. BRINGING UP BRAAP AND--

AND I GOT IT.
WOW. THAT WAS REALLY FAST.
I'M PRETTY GOOD AT THIS.
WE KNOW WHERE HE'S BEEN, SPIDEY...
"...WHICH TELLS US EXACTLY WHERE HE'S GOING."
OKAY, OKAY... HE'S GONE...
...I LOST HIM.
IF SHOCKER WAS GOING TO GO ROGUE, HE COULD HAVE AT LEAST LED SPIDER-MAN AND THE BLACK CAT AWAY.
PANTHER.
BLACK PANTHER.
I HAVE NO IDEA HOW YOU HAVE NOT HEARD OF ME.
YEAGH!

PANTHER'S GOT A POINT. YOU *HAVE* TO KEEP UP.
THIS ISN'T LIKE THE *OLD DAYS*, WHEN YOU WERE A KID--
--AND ALL YOU NEEDED TO COMMIT *ROBBERY* WAS A *HORSE* AND A *STAGECOACH TIMETABLE*.
NOWADAYS, YOU HAVE TO *PAY ATTENTION*.
YOU EVER HEAR OF THE *INTERNET?* TURNS OUT, IT'S REALLY *USEFUL*.
SPIDER-MAN, DO NOT GET *OVER-CONFIDENT*--
--THE *ARC REACTOR* HE STOLE COULD *BURN THROUGH* YOUR WEBS.
WHAT ARC REACTOR?
NEVER MIND. I'LL TAKE YOUR ADVICE AND *FRINGO* IT.
THAT IS, *AFTER* I USE SOMETHING I *DID* STEAL.
FIRST A *MINI ARC REACTOR*...
...NOW A *REPULSOR GENERATOR*.
LOOKS LIKE VULTURE'S TRYING TO BUILD HIS OWN *IRON MAN*.

I TRY SHOOTING ANOTHER WEBLINE TO STOP HIM--
--BUT VULTURE'S LITERALLY GONE BALLISTIC.
FOR HALF A SECOND, I'M ACTUALLY WORRIED ABOUT BLACK PANTHER.
BUT OF COURSE T'CHALLA HAS THE SITUATION WELL IN HAND.
OR CLAW.
THE POINT IS, IT'S REALLY SOMETHING TO SEE.

THAT WAS THE COOLEST THING EVER.
OUR WINGED FOE IS NEITHER DOWN NOR OUT...

"...AND HE STILL HAS STARK'S REPULSOR."
LATER DAYS, SPIDER-MAN!

FWOOOM

OH--

I GOTCHA.
IN FACT, THIS MIGHT JUST COME IN HANDY!
SEWER

MY CLOSE PERSONAL FRIEND CAPTAIN AMERICA TAUGHT ME A TRICK OR TWO.
BAD NEWS, VULTURE--YOU'RE GROUNDED!
PLONK
I DO NOT BELIEVE CAPTAIN AMERICA SHOWED YOU THAT PARTICULAR TECHNIQUE.
I'M A LITTLE OUT OF PRACTICE.
WAIT, PANTHER--YOU SURE YOU KNOW WHAT YOU'RE DOING?
OF COURSE YOU DO.
YOUR MASK PROBABLY BLOCKS THE SMELL...
...BUT MINE SURE DOESN'T.

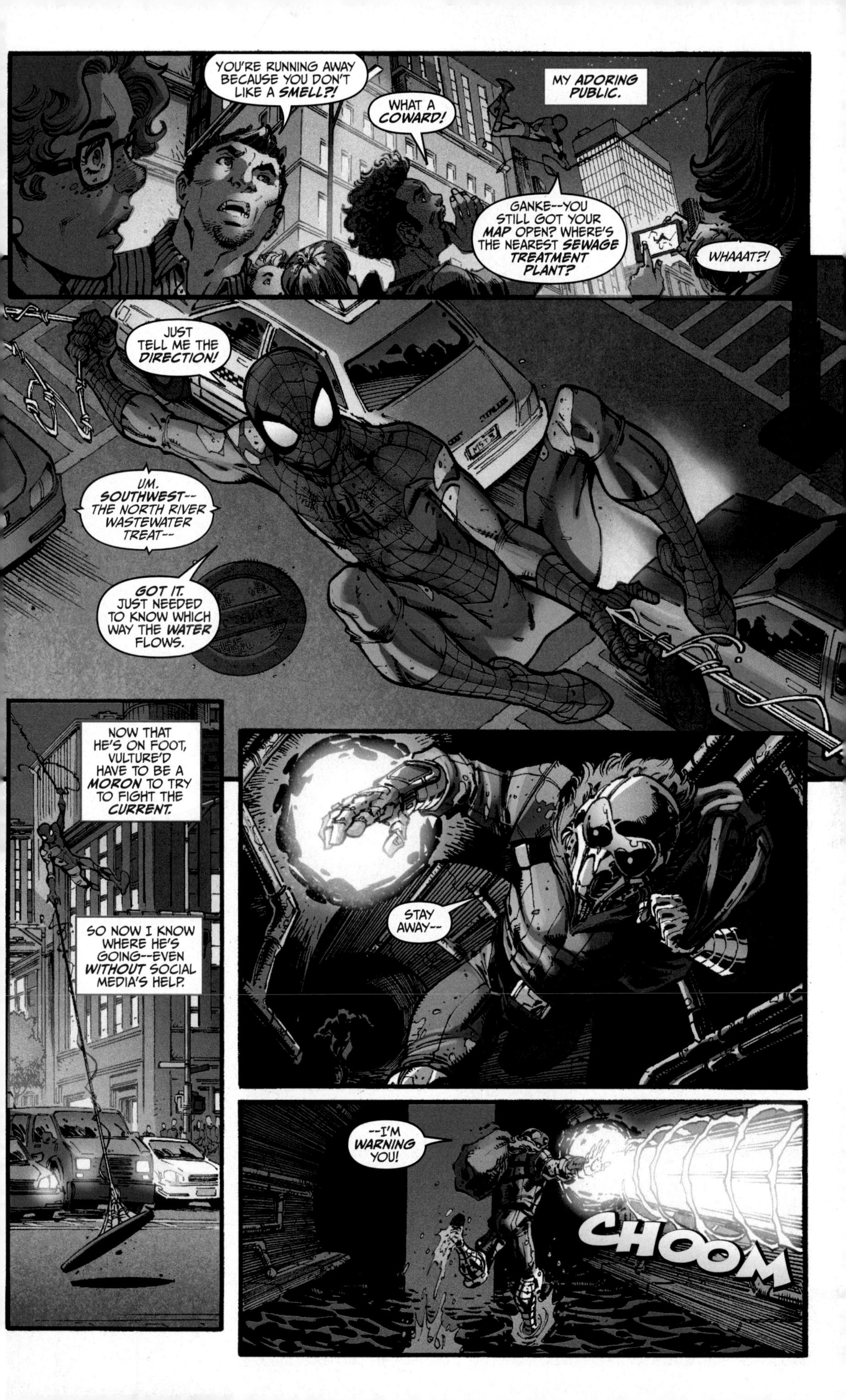
YOU'RE RUNNING AWAY BECAUSE YOU DON'T LIKE A SMELL?!
WHAT A COWARD!
MY ADORING PUBLIC.
GANKE--YOU STILL GOT YOUR MAP OPEN? WHERE'S THE NEAREST SEWAGE TREATMENT PLANT?
WHAAAT?!
JUST TELL ME THE DIRECTION!
UM. SOUTHWEST-- THE NORTH RIVER WASTEWATER TREAT--
GOT IT. JUST NEEDED TO KNOW WHICH WAY THE WATER FLOWS.
NOW THAT HE'S ON FOOT, VULTURE'D HAVE TO BE A MORON TO TRY TO FIGHT THE CURRENT.
SO NOW I KNOW WHERE HE'S GOING--EVEN WITHOUT SOCIAL MEDIA'S HELP.
STAY AWAY--
--I'M WARNING YOU!
CHOOM

THAT SHOULD SLOW HIM--
YOINK
MIND IF I BORROW THIS?
WAIT--
--I WAS JUST TRYING TO MAKE AN HONEST BUCK.
OUCH. WOW.
THAT'S... REALLY EFFICIENT, B.P.

ALL THE PIECES FALL INTO PLACE.
VULTURE AND SHOCKER GO WAY BACK. BALDY HERE SENT SHOCKER TO STARK CAMP TO STEAL EQUIPMENT.
SELLING SUPER HERO GEAR ON THE BLACK MARKET IS CLASSIC VULTURE.
GO ON.
WELL... I GUESS HE MADE GG'S HOLOGRAM PROJECTOR GO NUTS TO COVER THE THEFT OF THE ARC REACTOR...
...BUT IN TRUE VILLAIN FORM HE WASN'T SATISFIED. SO HE SENT RHINO AND SHOCKER TO KEEP ME OCCUPIED.
HE DIDN'T COUNT ON ME TAKING THEM DOWN, OR YOU BEING AT STARK CAMP AT ALL.
WHAT I DON'T KNOW IS HOW HE KNEW MY ECRET-SAY DENTITY-IAY. OR WHEN HE OR SHOCKER ARE GONNA SPILL THE BEANS.
OR WHO THOSE BEANS WILL BE SPILLED ON. OR HOW TO GET THE STAIN OF THE BEANS OUT OF THEIR CLOTHES.
YOUR METAPHOR IS BECOMING STRAINED, SPIDER-MAN.
HOLOGRAM? RHINO? WHAT ARE YOU TALKING ABOUT?
I'M A BUSINESSMAN. I TRIED TO TAKE SOME STUFF, AND I GOT CAUGHT. BOO-HOO.
NOBODY WAS HURT, AND I'M SURE TONY STARK HAS INSURANCE.
MAYBE THIS DOESN'T ADD UP.
THAT IS NOT YOUR PROBLEM. AT LEAST NOT FOR TONIGHT. GET SOME REST.
I WILL TAKE VULTURE TO THE AUTHORITIES. AND PROTECT YOUR ECRET-SAY. I ASSURE YOU, SPIDER-MAN... THINGS WILL LOOK BETTER IN THE MORNING.

PANTHER MADE A GOOD ARGUMENT.
PLUS, ONCE THE ADRENALINE WORE OFF, MY BODY MADE A GOOD ARGUMENT.
I GOT A SOLID FOUR HOURS OF SLEEP, IGNORING GANKE'S QUESTIONS...
...BEFORE I SLIPPED OUT TO VISIT THE MOST IMPORTANT PERSON IN MY LIFE.
AUNT MAY!
PETER! WHAT ARE YOU DOING HERE?!
AND WHAT HAPPENED TO YOUR EYE?
ARE YOU KIDDING? YOU'RE PRACTICALLY MY FAVORITE AUNT.
YOU OKAY?
AND I JUST BUMPED MY EYE ON... SOMETHING.
I'M FINE.
THE ONLY REASON THEY MADE ME STAY OVERNIGHT IS BECAUSE I LISTENED TO THAT DREADFUL SPIDER-MAN...
...AND TOLD THE PARAMEDIC I WAS UNCONSCIOUS FOR A FEW MINUTES.
WELL, THAT SOUNDS LIKE A GOOD IDEA. I'M GLAD YOU DID.
AND I'M SORRY I COULDN'T GET OVER TO SEE YOU LAST NIGHT, AUNT MAY.

DON'T BE SILLY. IT WAS A LUCKY THING YOU WERE AT CAMP.
THE HOUSE IS A WRECK. MRS. WATSON SAID SHE WAS KEEPING AN EYE ON IT, BUT IN THIS DAY AND AGE...
ANYWAY. HOPEFULLY I CAN GET SOMEONE OUT LATER TODAY TO GET TO WORK.
BY THE TIME YOU'RE HOME FROM CAMP, WE'LL BE BACK TO THE CORRECT NUMBER OF WALLS.
I--I'M NOT GOING BACK TO CAMP, AUNT MAY.
I'M GONNA TAKE YOU HOME AS SOON AS THE DOCTOR SAYS IT'S OKAY, AND--
WHAT ARE YOU TALKING ABOUT, PETER?
THIS WAS A TERRIBLE EXPERIENCE, BUT IT'S HARDLY THE WORST BRUSH WITH CRIME I'VE HAD.
WHEN LIFE KNOCKS YOU DOWN, YOU DON'T GIVE UP.
NO, IT'S FINE.
CAMP WASN'T ALL IT WAS CRACKED UP TO BE.
PETER PARKER.
YOUR UNCLE BEN AND I SCRIMPED AND SAVED OUR WHOLE LIVES SO YOU WOULD HAVE OPPORTUNITIES LIKE STARK CAMP.
THE WORLD NEEDS PEOPLE LIKE YOU--PEOPLE WHO USE BRAINS, NOT FISTS LIKE THOSE SUPER-HUMANS.
I GUESS...
...I GUESS THEY DO. THE WORLD, I MEAN. NEEDS ME, THAT IS.
AT LEAST AUNT MAY HAS A WAY OF PUTTING THINGS NICELY.

I STAY FOR AN HOUR, LISTENING TO HER STORY.
FINALLY AUNT MAY INSISTS I GET TO CAMP BEFORE I GET MARKED TARDY--
--WHICH INDICATES SHE MAYBE DOESN'T GET HOW CAMP ACTUALLY WORKS, BUT HER OVERALL POINT REMAINS.
I REALLY WASN'T EXPECTING WHAT I SAW NEXT.
WHAT ARE YOU DOING HERE?
HEY, PETE. MRS. LIU TOLD US YOU'D PROBABLY BE HERE. WE WANTED TO MAKE SURE YOU WERE OKAY.
YO.
AND HARRY AND I WANTED TO CHECK IN ON AUNT MAY. SHE'S LIKE FAMILY TO US, TOO.
WE SAW YOU WERE IN THERE AND WE'VE JUST BEEN LOITERING WITH YOUR NEW FRIENDS.
STARK
GWEN, I'M SO GLAD TO SEE YOU.
I MISSED YOU SO MUCH.
UGH. PUBLIC DISPLAYS OF AFFECTION.
WOW.
UGH.
STARK
MY DAD'S A BIG CONTRIBUTOR TO THE HOSPITAL, SO, YOU KNOW, THEY LET US HANG AROUND.

H, HEY. GANKE, G--THESE ARE FRIENDS GWEN ACY AND HARRY OSBORN.
AHEM.
MY GIRLFRIEND GWEN! SORRY. I'M STILL NOT USED TO THAT.
WAIT, NORMAN OSBORN'S SON? WOW WOW!
I FIGURED YOU'D FORGET YOU WERE MY BOYFRIEND THE SECOND YOU WENT TO CAMP.
HEH. HE'S HAD OTHER THINGS KEEPING HIM BUSY.
IF YOU KNOW WHAT I MEAN.
UH. NOT REALLY...?
HOMEWORK. THE BIG PROJECT. LOTS OF SCIENCE.
WE'VE BEEN BUSY.
STARK
SHE DOESN'T KNOW.

OH! YEAH! WHY NOT? I MEAN--
PLUS THERE WAS A BREAK-IN AND--
AND ALL KINDS OF STUFF.

WHICH WE BETTER GET BACK TO IF WE DON'T WANT MRS. LIU GETTING MAD AT US.

HEH. YEAH. BYE, GWEN, HARRY!
I'LL BE HOME SOON.

I'M VERY HAPPY YOU'RE STAYING.
AND I'M RELIEVED YOUR AUNT IS OKAY.
SHE'S MORE THAN THAT. SHE'S REALLY SOMETHING.
IF YOU'D HAVE COME TO ME, I COULD HAVE ARRANGED A CAR OR--
IT'S OKAY, MRS. LIU. I LIKE GOING AROUND THE CITY THE OLD-FASHIONED WAY.
NOW WE'RE DOWN TO THE HOME STRETCH OF STARK CAMP.
I HOPE YOUR FINAL PROJECT WILL LIVE UP TO THE POTENTIAL YOUR APPLICATION SHOWED.
YEAH...FINAL PROJECT.
IS IT GOING WELL?
IT'S GOING GREAT.
AS SOON AS I FIGURE OUT WHAT IT IS.
ANNNND...THAT'S THE LIFE OF A SUPER HERO.
SAVED THE DAY, MY SECRET IDENTITY IS PROBABLY BLOWN, MY LIFE AS I KNOW IT IS INCHES FROM BEING OVER...
...SO TIME TO WORRY ABOUT THE STUFF NORMAL KIDS DO.
BUT I GUESS IT'S NOT ALL BAD. AUNT MAY TALKED ABOUT WHAT A GREAT OPPORTUNITY IT IS TO BE HERE...

...AN OPPORTUNITY I WOULDN'T HAVE UNLESS TONY STARK FIGURED OUT I'M...
TONY STARK?
ACTUALLY, I WAS GOING TO SAY "SPIDER-MAN," BUT WHAT'S TONY DOING HERE?
(ALSO, NOW THAT HE'S FIGURED OUT MY SECRET IDENTITY, ARE WE AT THE "TONY" OR "MR. STARK" PHASE OF OUR RELATIONSHIP?)
MAYBE HE WANTS TO THANK ME FOR SAVING HIS CAMP.
WAIT, I FORGOT WHO I AM.
HE PROBABLY WANTS TO YELL AT ME FOR NOT LEAVING EVERYTHING TO THE PANTHER.
TONY? OR, UH, MR. STARK?
WHAT'S UP?

TIME, MR. PARKER.
TIME IS UP.
HELP.
STARK
W-WHAT'S GOING ON HERE?
GANKE-- ARE YOU OKAY?
CHOOM

6

THAT'S ME.
AND THAT'S IRON MAN'S REPULSOR BEAM.
OUCH, RIGHT?
STARK
YOU SHOT PETE! IRON MAN JUST KILLED PETER PARKER!
WHY IS ALL THIS HAPPENING!?
SHUT IT. YOU WOULDN'T UNDERSTAND.
WUMP
STARK
OOF!
TELL YOUR GOONS TO LET GO OF ME!

TIMES LIKE THIS, I'M LUCKY I'M SPIDER-MAN. IF I WERE A NORMAL KID, THAT WOULD HAVE KNOCKED ME OUT--OR WORSE.
UT IT ADDS UP. ALL EEK, SOMEBODY'S EEN USING PETER PARKER TO GO FTER SPIDER-MAN.
ONY "IRON MAN" STARK KNOWS I'M SPIDEY-- I'M SURE THAT'S WHY HE INVITED ME TO HIS CAMP, AFTER ALL.
IT ADDS UP...EXCEPT FOR THE WHY.
PETER? ARE YOU OKAY? WHAT'S HAPPENING?
GET EVERYBODY OUT OF HERE, NEEL. THINGS ARE GOING BANANAS AGAIN.
OW IS HE STILL STANDING?
A FULL-FORCE REPULSOR BLAST SHOULD HAVE PUT HIM DOWN FOR HOURS.
WELL, YOU DON'T KNOW WHO YOU'RE MESSING WITH!
PETER PARKER'S JUST A STUPID POOR KID.
WEIRD. STARK'S NOT LETTING ON ABOUT MY IDENTITY...
...PLUS, HE DOESN'T SOUND LIKE THE TONY STARK I KNOW.
WELL, SORT OF KNOW.
MET ONCE, ANYWAY.
BUT WE TEAMED UP! WE HAD A THING GOING!

function projectBricks() {
I GUESS PEOPLE ARE FULL OF SURPRISES.
var brickX =
(r*(brickWidth+brickPadding))+brickOffsetLeft;
var brickY =
(c*(brickHeight+brickPadding))+brickOffsetTop;
bricks[c][r].x = brickX;
bricks[c][r].y = brickY;
ctx.beginPath();
ctx.rect(brickX, brickY, brickWidth, brickHeight);
ctx.repulsorStrength = "4forcelumens"
ctx.closePath();
TONY STARK'S CHASING PETER!
THAT'S THE STUPIDEST THING I'VE EVER HEARD!
CAN YOU TWO KEEP IT DOWN?
I'M TRYING TO WORK, AND I DON'T CARE IF PARKER'S GOT HIMSELF IN TROUBLE.
GG, YOU DON'T UNDERSTAND-- IT'S NOT JUST STARK!
YOU SAID IT WAS!
YOU DIDN'T LET ME FINISH, RIYA! IT'S IRON MAN!
WHAT?
HE'S GOT TWO OTHER...I DON'T KNOW, IRON MEN WITH HIM. THEY'RE BLASTING EVERYTHING AND THEY'RE HOLDING GANKE HOSTAGE!
SHOW ME WHERE, AND LET'S FIGURE OUT WHAT TO DO.
WE CAN'T ALWAYS RELY ON--
--SUPER HEROES SHOWING UP ON CUE.
UH. HI, THERE.

HAPPENED TO BE IN THE NEIGHBORHOOD. AGAIN.
AND WHAT DO YOU KNOW, IRON MAN TURNED EVIL OR SOMETHING.
IT'S A LITTLE BIT LIKE GOOD LUCK, I GUESS.
NOW--YOU, AH, KIDS GET OUT OF HERE. I CAN HANDLE THIS ALONE.
BECAUSE THAT'S GONE GREAT. RHINO AND SHOCKER ALMOST STOMPED ME WHEN I COULD'VE HAD BLACK PANTHER ON MY SIDE.
AND I'D HAVE NEVER BEEN ABLE TO STOP SHOCKER THE FIRST TIME WITHOUT GG'S HELP.
OH NO. DON'T TELL ME I'M ACTUALLY GROWING AS A PERSON.
HANG ON. SCRATCH THAT.
NEEL, RIYA-- I NEED YOU TO GET EVERYBODY TO SAFETY. THIS HAS THE POTENTIAL TO GO BIG-TIME WRONG.
GG--
--I HAVE A PLAN.

WHAT DO YOU WANT FROM ME?! I'M JUST A KID THAT LIKES COMPUTERS AND COMIC BOOKS!
STARK
WRONG. YOU'RE BAIT, GANKE LEE.
WE THROW YOU OUT AND REEL IN PETER PARKER.
THAT DOESN'T MAKE ANY-- AIIGH!
SPLATT
AIIGH!
SPIDER-MAN!
WHY DO YOU KEEP SHOWING UP?!
FZZARRT
JUST GET HIM!

CHOOM CHOOM
SPIDER-MAN! CALL THE AVENGERS!
GET HELP!
DON'T WORRY, UM, SON! HELP IS ON THE WAY.
THEY'RE JUST TRYING TO GET AWAY FROM ME, NOT FIGHT ME. WHICH IS, ON ONE HAND, A WELCOME BREAK FROM MONOTONY...
CHOOM
...BUT WHY GO AFTER PETER AND NOT SPIDEY--IF THEY KNOW WE'RE BOTH ME?!*
GG, THIS IS SPIDER-MAN. DO YOU READ ME?
*THAT GOT CONVOLUTED, BUT YOU KNOW WHAT I MEAN.
YIKES, I.M.!
I KNOW WE'RE NOT BESTIES OR ANYTHING, BUT HAVEN'T WE MOVED PAST THE "TRY TO BLAST ME TO ATOMS" PHASE OF OUR RELATIONSHIP?
WHO ELSE WOULD BE CALLING ME ON GANKE'S HEADPHONES?
I ACCESSED STARK'S PROJECTION GRID AND PULLED ENOUGH STUDENT PHOTOS FROM THE CAMP SERVER TO MAKE A 3D MODEL.
BUT BELIEVE IT OR NOT, I DON'T HAVE THE RIGHT WIREFRAME TO MAP THE MODEL ONTO.
I NEED SOMETHING I CAN PROJECT--
I'VE GOT IT ALL FIGURED OUT.
WELL, "ALL" MIGHT BE A STRETCH, BUT I'M CONFIDENT SOMETHING WILL COME TOGETHER.

YOU KNOW, USUALLY STARK CAMP IS STRESSFUL BECAUSE WE ALL HAVE TO PRESENT OUR DEALS--
--NOT BECAUSE ARMORED MANIACS ARE DRAGGING US THROUGH THE HALLS!
QUIET.
YOU'RE NOT THE BOSS OF HIM.
WHO--?
LET GANKE GO...
...I HEAR IT'S ME YOU'RE LOOKING FOR.
I KNEW YOU WERE UNDERPRIVILEGED, PARKER--BUT YOU'RE ALSO A MASSIVE IDIOT.
CHOOM
PETE! NOT AGAIN!
OH YEAH--
--AGAIN.
FWUMP

I DON'T KNOW WHAT TRICK YOU'RE PULLING--
--BUT IT'S GONNA BE A LONG TIME BEFORE I GET TIRED OF BLASTING PETER PARKERS.
WELL, I GOTTA ADMIT...
...THAT'S A RELIEF.
ALSO, I THINK GRAMMATICALLY IT'S "PETERS PARKER."
THESE ARE JUST HOLOGRAMS. HE'S TRYING TO FOOL US.
I TOLD YOU YOU DIDN'T KNOW WHO YOU WERE MESSING WITH!
LET'S TRY TO KEEP IT THAT WAY.
PETE! WHAT DOES THAT MEAN?
IT MEANS SHHHH--
STARK

--BE QUIET AND TRY TO BLEND IN.
HEY! WHAT ARE YOU--
--AW, MAN.
WHICH ONE?!
WHO CARES. BLAST 'EM ALL!
CHOOM
CHOOM
CHOOM

GG--THIS IS SPIDER-MAN.
OKAY, OKAY, YOU KNOW WHO I AM.
GANKE AND THAT PARKER KID ARE SAFE.
GOOD. RIYA JUST TEXTED--SHE AND HER BROTHER GOT EVERYBODY ELSE OUT.
I'VE HACKED THE HOLOGRAM NETWORK, BUT I'M NOT ALONE. SOMEBODY ELSE IS USING THE PROJECTORS TO--
FZZT
SPIDER-MAN? DO YOU READ ME?
LOST CONTACT WITH GG. THEY'RE JAMMING US. MUST HAVE FIGURED OUT WE WERE JUST USING CELL PHONES.
WHAT WERE YOU SAYING ABOUT HOLOGRAMS?
THIS WHOLE BUILDING IS LINED WITH PROJECTORS. THAT'S HOW HOLOGRAM TONY COULD GIVE US A PEP TALK.*
* BACK IN ISSUE #1!
"TONY." HA. SUPER HEROES CALLING EACH OTHER BY THEIR FIRST NAMES.
GANKE, THIS IS SUPER IMPORTANT--IF THE BAD GUYS JAMMED CELL RECEPTION, THEY'LL FIGURE OUT HOW TO BLOCK US FROM THE HOLOGRAM NETWORK.
I NEED YOU TO GET TO GG AND TELL HER I'M TAKING THEM TO THE BIG ROOM. SHE'LL KNOW WHAT TO DO.
YOU CAN COUNT ON ME!
I MAKE FUN OF "PARKER LUCK," BUT I'VE GOT THE BEST FRIENDS A GUY DRESSED LIKE A RED-AND-BLUE SPIDER CAN EVER HOPE TO HAVE.

ALSO, I HAVE SOME PERSISTENT ENEMIES.
SPIDER-MAN-- YOU'RE WASTING ALL OUR TIME.
YOU DON'T HAVE BLACK PANTHER TO HELP YOU ANYMORE.
MAYBE NOT--
--BUT THAT DOESN'T MEAN I'M ALONE.
ENOUGH OF THIS-- WE DIDN'T COME HERE TO FIGHT SPIDER-MAN--
--ESPECIALLY NOT A HOLOGRAM ARMY OF HIM.
WAIT, WHAT ARE YOU DOING?
GG! PETE-GOT-AWAY-BUT-THEY-JAMMED-THE-CELL-PHONES-AND-SPIDER-MAN-TOLD-ME-TO-TELL-YOU-THEY'RE-GOING-TO-THE-BIG-ROOM.
BREATHE, GANKE. WHOEVER THESE GUYS ARE, THEY'RE CREATING SOME KIND OF POWER SURGE--
"--BLOWING OUT THE NETWORK'S CAPACITORS...
POP
POP
POP
"...BUT I'VE GOT THIS HANDLED."
GAME OVER, SPIDER-MAN--

--NO MORE HOLOGRAMS.
LET'S FINISH THIS.
I SERIOUSLY THOUGHT WE WERE GOING TO GET INTO AN ARGUMENT NOW, BUT I GOTTA ADMIT--
--THAT SOUNDS LIKE A GOOD PLAN!
THWIP
AGH! GET HIM!
SETTLE DOWN. EVEN WITHOUT OUR HOLOGRAM IRON MAN, WE'RE STILL PLUGGED INTO THE MINI ARC REACTOR--
--AND THAT MEANS OUR REPULSORS CAN GO ALL DAY LONG!
CHOOM
CHOOM
LET'S SEE IF SPIDER-MAN CAN DO THE SAME!

CHOOM
WHAT?!
ANOTHER HOLOGRAM--
--BUT HOW DID--
YOU BLEW OUT THE STARK CENTER NETWORK--THE ONE PROJECTING YOUR ARMOR.
BUT YOU FORGOT ABOUT GG'S PROJECTOR...
...AND YOU FORGOT TO NOT LITERALLY ANNOUNCE THAT YOU'RE ONLY ABLE TO DO ANYTHING BECAUSE YOU'RE CONNECTED TO A POWER SOURCE YOU STOLE.
CHECK-YOINK.*
*LIKE CHECKMATE? GET IT? DOES THAT WORK?

SKRASHH
ALL RIGHT, KIDS. NOBODY MOVE.
THE ADULT'S HERE AND THIS SITUATION--
--IS ALREADY WELL IN HAND.
SPIDEY. FANCY MEETING YOU HERE.
FRIENDS OF YOURS?
NOT EXACTLY. MEET ETHAN AND LACHLAN, CREATORS OF THE KILLBLAST TRIGGER MOBILE APP.
TWO LONG-TIME STARK CAMPERS WHO SEEM TO HAVE DECIDED THIS YEAR WAS--
YEAH, YEAH, I REMEMBER THEM--
--THEIR PARENTS ARE BIG NEW YORK MOVERS AND SHAKERS. REAL DRIPS, IF YOU ASK ME.
THESE TWO SEEMED SMART, SO I FIGURED I'D GIVE THEM A CHANCE AT DOING SOMETHING GOOD IN LIFE.
WHY'D YOU THROW IT AWAY, KIDS?
COME ON. WE'RE IN IT FOR THE MONEY.
MICRO-TRANSACTIONS CAN MAKE YOU MILLIONS OF DOLLARS--BUT WE WERE GONNA HAVE TONY STARK'S INVENTORY WITHOUT THE MORALS HOLDING HIM BACK.
WE'D MAKE BILLIONS.

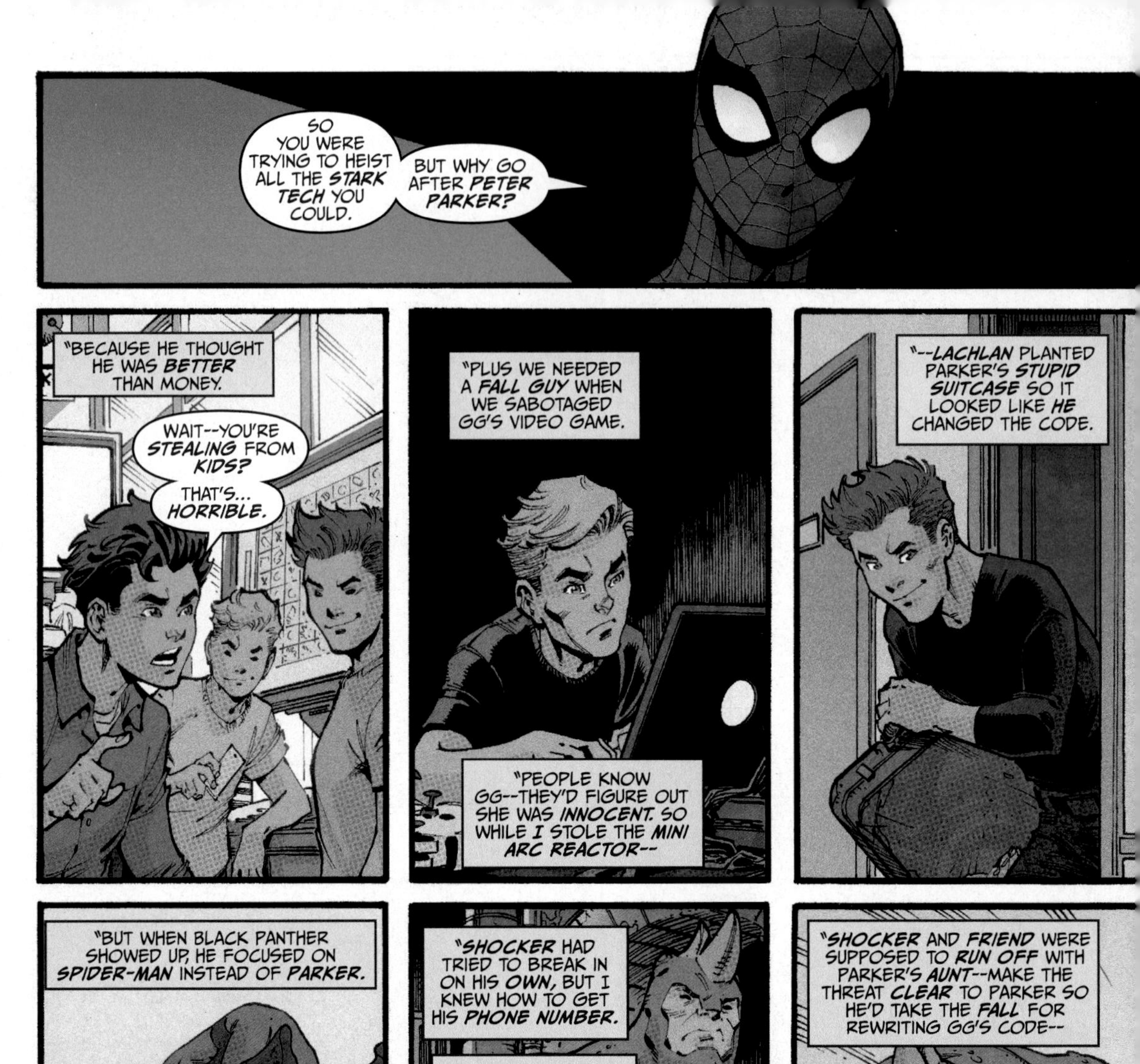
SO YOU WERE TRYING TO HEIST ALL THE STARK TECH YOU COULD.
BUT WHY GO AFTER PETER PARKER?
"BECAUSE HE THOUGHT HE WAS BETTER THAN MONEY.
WAIT--YOU'RE STEALING FROM KIDS?
THAT'S... HORRIBLE.
"PLUS WE NEEDED A FALL GUY WHEN WE SABOTAGED GG'S VIDEO GAME.
"PEOPLE KNOW GG--THEY'D FIGURE OUT SHE WAS INNOCENT. SO WHILE I STOLE THE MINI ARC REACTOR--
"--LACHLAN PLANTED PARKER'S STUPID SUITCASE SO IT LOOKED LIKE HE CHANGED THE CODE.

"BUT WHEN BLACK PANTHER SHOWED UP, HE FOCUSED ON SPIDER-MAN INSTEAD OF PARKER.
"THAT GOT ME EVEN MADDER AT THAT PARKER CHUMP.
"SHOCKER HAD TRIED TO BREAK IN ON HIS OWN, BUT I KNEW HOW TO GET HIS PHONE NUMBER.
"MY DAD'S A LAWYER. HE WORKS WITH SOME UNSAVORY CHARACTERS.
YEAH, I KNOW A GUY.
"SHOCKER AND FRIEND WERE SUPPOSED TO RUN OFF WITH PARKER'S AUNT--MAKE THE THREAT CLEAR TO PARKER SO HE'D TAKE THE FALL FOR REWRITING GG'S CODE--
"--BUT SOMEBODY TIPPED OFF THE COPS..."
...AND I GUESS VULTURE HAPPENED TO BE AROUND TO TAKE ADVANTAGE OF THE CONFUSION.
WAIT WAIT WAIT.
YOU WENT AFTER PARKER JUST BECAUSE HE THOUGHT YOUR APP RIPPED OFF KIDS?
THAT'S THE WAY OF THE WORLD SPIDEY...

"...SMART CRIMINALS DONE IN BY THEIR DUMB EGOS."
SO THE VULTURE STUFF WAS JUST COINCIDENCE.
YOU'RE KIDDING.
NOPE--THESE TWO KIDS WANTED TO BECOME A DARK VERSION OF ME, AND DECIDED TO GO AFTER SOME CLASSMATE NAMED PALMER.
PARKER. PETER PARKER. AND SPEAK OF THE DEVIL.
HI, MR. STARK.
YOU GOT A MINUTE?
SURE, KID. SEEMS LIKE YOU WENT THROUGH THE WRINGER.
MRS. LIU TELLS ME YOUR AUNT GOT HURT BECAUSE OF ALL THIS. I'M REALLY SORRY.
GOOD THING SPIDER-MAN WAS AROUND.

IT SURE WAS, MR. STARK. WINK WINK.
WHY DID YOU JUST SAY "WINK WINK" OUT LOUD?
BECAUSE THE ONLY REASON I'M HERE IS SPIDER-MAN.

KID, DON'T TAKE THIS THE WRONG WAY, BUT I DON'T KNOW WHAT YOU'RE TALKING ABOUT.
NOBODY'S AROUND. YOU DON'T HAVE TO PRETEND YOU DON'T KNOW WHO I AM, MR. STARK.
WHY WOULD I KNOW YOU?

HANG ON. YOU'RE SAYING YOU ACCEPTED ME TO STARK CAMP BECAUSE OF--
YOUR APPLICATION. YOUR GRADES. TEACHER RECOMMENDATIONS.
SAME AS EVERYBODY ELSE.

WOW. THANKS, MR. STARK.
THAT'S THE COOLEST THING THAT'S HAPPENED ALL WEEK.
SO THIS WASN'T A SPIDER-MAN ADVENTURE.

EXCEPT FOR THE PARTS THAT WERE, LIKE WHEN I SHOT WEBS INTO RHINO'S MOUTH.
BUT OTHERWISE, THIS WAS A PETER PARKER ADVENTURE.
WE CAN'T ALWAYS RELY ON SUPER HEROES SHOWING UP ON CUE.
WE HAVE PROBLEMS EVERY DAY. WHEN IT'S A ROBBERY OR A FIRE, WE KNOW TO CALL THE COPS OR THE FIRE DEPARTMENT.
BUT WHAT IF YOU LOSE YOUR KEYS, OR YOU NEED SOMEBODY WHO CAN WRITE A COMPUTER ALGORITHM TO FIND YOUR...PET BIRD OR WHATEVER?
MY D-SENSE APP LETS US ALL HELP EACH OTHER.
BECAUSE MAYBE YOU KNOW HOW TO BUILD A BETTER WALL, OR A BETTER COMPUTER, OR A BETTER GENETIC... THING.
THE D IN D-SENSE IS FOR "DOING"...

...BECAUSE LIFE'S ABOUT DOING SOMETHING TO HELP YOUR FELLOW HUMAN BEINGS.
EVERYBODY WHO JOINS THE D-SENSE NETWORK IS PLEDGING THEY'LL HELP PEOPLE-- AND THAT THEY'LL ACCEPT HELP IN RETURN.
NOT EVERY PROBLEM NEEDS A SUPER HERO...
...BUT WHEN YOU DO, I HAVE IT ON GOOD AUTHORITY THAT SPIDER-MAN WILL BE CHECKING D-SENSE REGULARLY.
BECAUSE HE'S JUST LIKE THE REST OF US--
--DOING HIS BEST TO HELP EVERYBODY HE CAN.

THAT WAS A REALLY COOL PROJECT TO PULL TOGETHER AT THE *LAST MINUTE,* PETE.
YEAH, WELL, I WAS *INSPIRED.* THANKS FOR YOUR *HELP,* GANKE.
ANY TIME, PETE.
YOU'LL *FRINGO* ME BEFORE SUMMER'S OVER, RIGHT?
YOU *BET.*
GREAT. YOU NEED TO MEET MY *BEST FRIEND* FROM SCHOOL--*MILES.*
YOU GUYS WOULD *REALLY* GET ALONG.
HONK
THAT'S MY *MOM.* GOTTA GO!
GANKE LEE
GIZMON
YOU'RE NOT EXPECTING A *HUG,* ARE YOU?
STARK
CONGRATS ON TAKING *FIRST PLACE,* GG. YOU REALLY *DESERVED* IT.
IF IT WEREN'T FOR *YOU,* SPIDER--
ANSWER YOUR *PHONE,* PARKER.
GG--WAIT, I--
FORGET IT.
BEEP
HELLO?

PETER! IT'S ME, HARRY!
AND GWEN!
AND GWEN. WE'RE WITH YOUR AUNT!
WHAT HAPPENED?! IS SHE OKAY?
TARK
MAY'S MAD SHE HAD TO GET WHEELED OUT OF THE HOSPITAL WHEN SHE'S, QUOTE, PERFECTLY CAPABLE OF WALKING--BUT SHE'S FINE.
THE PROBLEM IS WE'RE STUCK AT THE HOSPITAL AND CAN'T PICK YOU UP.
WHAT'S WRONG?
SOME KIND OF SUPER-GUY IS AFTER A MOB INFORMER OR SOMETHING.
THE WHOLE HOSPITAL IS ON LOCKDOWN. WE'RE GONNA BE STUCK HERE FOR HOURS.
IT'S A LITTLE SCARY...

RELAX, GWEN.
JUST LOOK AFTER MAY AND HARRY--
--I'M SURE HELP IS ON THE WAY.
I WAS HOPING MY NEXT PETER PARKER ADVENTURE WOULD BE A WEEK OF NONSTOP SLEEP, BUT WHEN PEOPLE ARE COUNTING ON ME...
...WELL, THERE ARE WORSE PROBLEMS TO HAVE.
AND WORSE PEOPLE TO BE THAN YOUR FRIENDLY NEIGHBORHOOD
SPIDEY
END.

SKETCHES BY TODD NAUCK

#1 LAYOUTS

BY TODD NAUCK

#2 LAYOUTS

BY TODD NAUCK

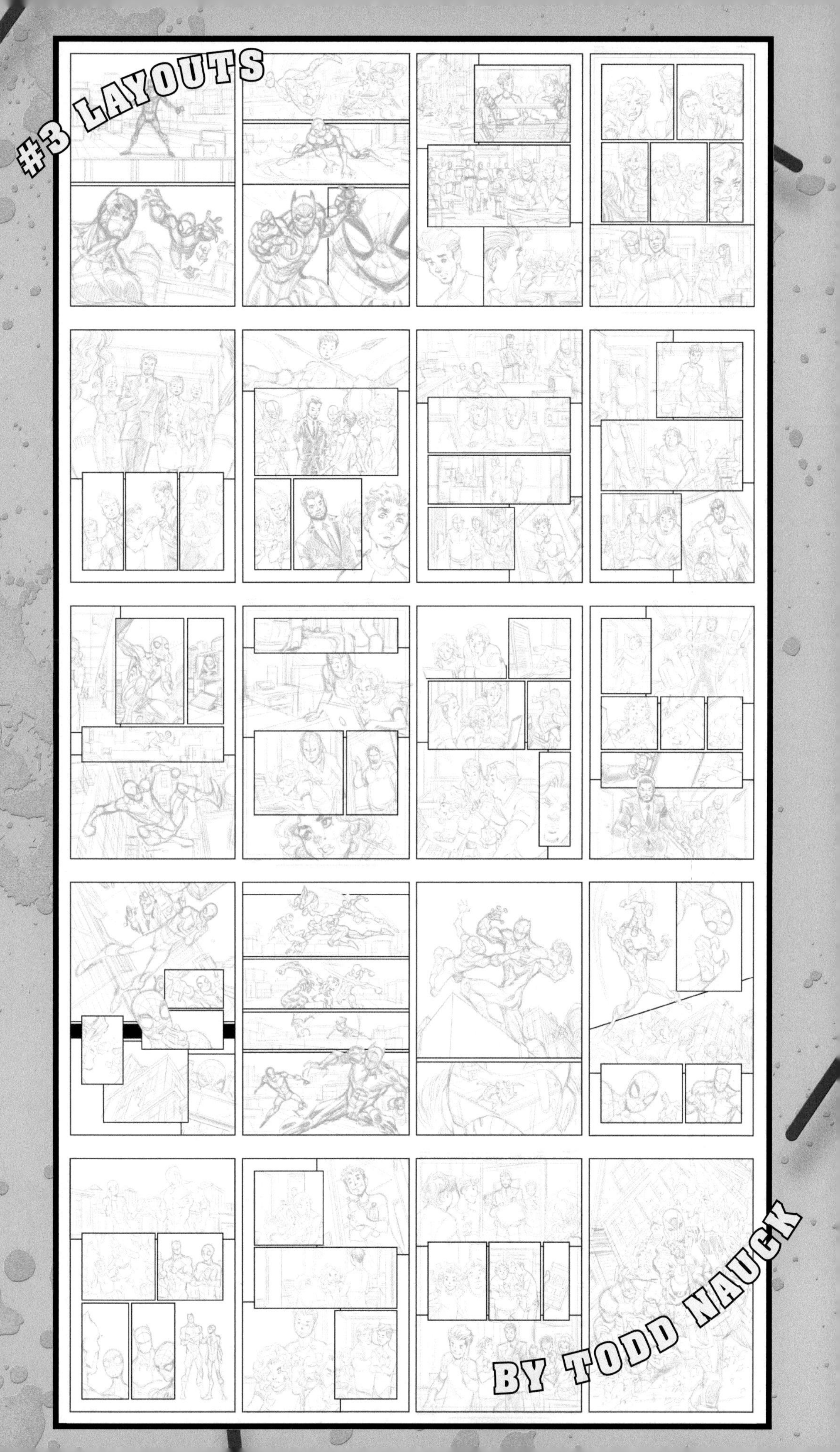
#3 LAYOUTS
BY TODD NAUCK

#4 LAYOUTS

BY TODD NAUCK

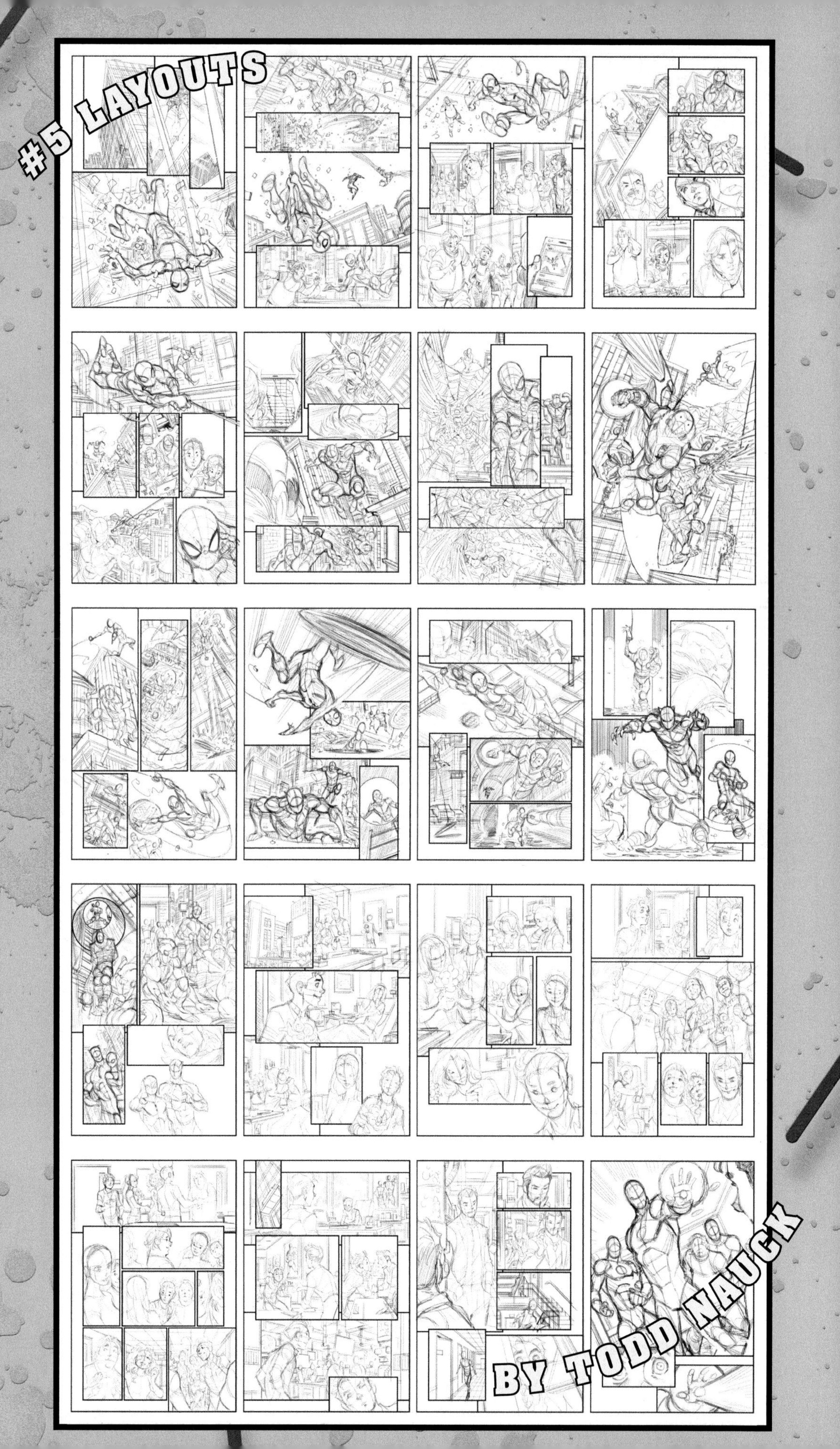
#5 LAYOUTS
BY TODD NAUCK

#6 LAYOUTS

BY TODD NAUCK